PAVANE

by
Sally Dixon Wiener

To the men in my life, for their continuing support.
John A. Wiener and John Dixon Wiener
It was love at first sight, in both instances.

Off Off Broadway Festival Plays

Twentieth Series

PAVANE
by Sally Dixon Wiener

THE ART OF DATING
by Jeffrey Scott Elwell

SNOW STARS
by Anne V. Sawyer

LIFE COMES TO THE OLD MAID
by Le Wilhelm

THE APPOINTMENT
by Luigi Jannuzzi

A WINTER REUNION
by Henry Miller

A SAMUEL FRENCH ACTING EDITION

SAMUELFRENCH.COM
SAMUELFRENCH-LONDON.CO.UK

ISBN 978-0-573-60248-1
www.SamuelFrench.com
www.SamuelFrench-London.co.uk

FOR PRODUCTION ENQUIRIES

UNITED STATES AND CANADA
Info@SamuelFrench.com
1-866-598-8449

UNITED KINGDOM AND EUROPE
Theatre@SamuelFrench-London.co.uk
020-7255-4302

Each title is subject to availability from Samuel French, depending upon country of performance. Please be aware that *PAVANE, THE ART OF DATING, SNOW STARS, LIFE COMES TO THE OLD MAID, THE APPOINTMENT,* and *A WINTER REUNION* may not be licensed by Samuel French in your territory. Professional and amateur producers should contact the nearest Samuel French office or licensing partner to verify availability.

MUSIC USE NOTE

IMPORTANT BILLING AND CREDIT REQUIREMENTS

TABLE OF CONTENTS

PAVANE 5

THE ART OF DATING 45

SNOW STARS 69

LIFE COMES TO THE OLD MAID 81

THE APPOINTMENT 95

A WINTER REUNION 121

PAVANE was originally presented for four performances September 17, 18 and 19, 1994 as part of Love Creek Productions' Gay and Lesbian One Act Festival at The Nat Horne Theatre, Theatre Row, New York City. Helen Diane Hoblit was the director and the cast was as follows:

HARRY . . . . Don Jeffrey
NORMA . . . . Sharon Prince*
ABBEY . . . . Edythe Davis*
OLIVER . . . . Edmund Wilkinson*

PAVANE was subsequently presented May 15 and 21, 1995 by Love Creek Productions for The 20th Annual Off-Off-Broadway Short Play Festival at The Harold Clurman Theatre, Theatre Row, New York City. Sharon Fallon was the director and the cast was as follows:

HARRY . . . . Jeffrey J. Albright*
NORMA . . . . Donna Davidge*
ABBEY . . . . Pamela J. Nigro*
OLIVER . . . . Edmund Wilkinson*

ABOUT THE AUTHOR

Sally Dixon Wiener has had two dozen plus productions of her plays and musicals in New York and elsewhere, including eight premieres at Love Creek on 42nd Street's Theatre Row. A Carmel CA Festival of Firsts winner, Stanley Drama Award finalist and semi-finalist, she has had plays published by Samuel French, Inc. and others. She is a member of The League of Professional Theatre Women/NY, Dramatists Guild and The Writers Room.

Appearing through the courtesy of Actors' Equity Association

CHARACTERS:

HARRY: Tall and thoughtful, 41.

NORMA: Nurturing and solid, 39.

ABBEY: Norma's partner, poetic and sensitive, 35.

OLIVER: Harry's partner, a witty, wry skeptic, 38.

TIME & PLACE:

Spring of the present year and, in memory, the preceding four years. Various locations in an East Coast urban area.

Author's note: Although the script remains unchanged, *Pavane* was originally conceived as a readers' theatre work, a tale to be told by actors holding bound scripts, seated on high stools or in chairs at each end of a rectangular table, the two women to one side, the two men to the other side – á la Shaw's *Don Juan in Hell* or A.R. Gurney's *Love Letters*. Non-traditional casting is, of course, encouraged in any event.

PAVANE

(The play takes place in various locations, but it is best served by being performed in a simple setting. Four matching easy-to-handle chairs suffice to create the world of the four characters. One speech may sometimes overlap with the preceding one as long as clarity is considered. As the title implies, the play is to be played in a manner that is reminiscent of the ancient formal court dance for couples – and with an elegiac feeling and a deep and abiding tenderness between all four. Music, a pavane, the Fauré preferably, would fade out as the play begins. The lights come up on HARRY, tall and thoughtful, 41; NORMA, nurturing and solid, 39; ABBEY, poetic and sensitive, 35; and OLIVER, a witty, wry skeptic, 38. The time is the present, the spring of the present year, and, in memory, the preceding four years. The place is an East Coast urban area.)

HARRY: A story.

NORMA: Not an old story.

ABBEY: Not to us ... Not yet ...

OLIVER: *(looking out at the audience with a shrug, a so-what's-new look and nod)* "A fairy story."

HARRY: No. "Fairy stories are unbelievable."

ABBEY: And/or untrue.

NORMA: This was true.

ABBEY: Too true.

OLIVER: Okay. You're right.

HARRY: "A fairy. An imaginary being. Usually in human form. With magic powers. And specifically one that's tiny, graceful –"

NORMA: Well?

OLIVER: "– and delicate."

HARRY: Don't, please! ... Or I –

OLIVER: We have to, before –

NORMA: It's the only way we –

ABBEY: *(to HARRY)* You promised.

OLIVER: And the other definition is, of course, the obvious term of contempt. Quaint!

ABBEY: But fairyland itself can be –

NORMA: – an imaginary land –

OLIVER: – where fairies live.

ABBEY: Or!

HARRY: Any lovely enchanted place like, like – Oh, God ...

(He looks around.)

OLIVER: Go on!

HARRY: *(remembering)* Once upon a time – It was spring.

NORMA: Yes. That's how it begins.

OLIVER: Began ... Four years ago.

ABBEY: That incredible spring. First the snowdrops, then the crocus –

OLIVER: Daffodils, grape hyacinths, the magnolia –

NORMA: The tulips –

OLIVER: Pear trees, the cherry trees, and all the –

ABBEY: The wisteria. And every evening –

HARRY: We walked and talked and –

NORMA: Couple by couple –

ABBEY: That time of the year the earth seems to make its own music and –

HARRY: It was like dancing –

OLIVER: Like dancing a – a pavane ...

ABBEY: We sighed and dreamed, and drowned in the skyful of blossoms that fell onto –

NORMA: Our hair –

OLIVER: Our eyelids –

HARRY: Our hands. And up above, in that tender blue sky –

OLIVER: That blue that April cradles the world in –

ABBEY: That special blue, yes –

HARRY: Up in that sky there was a new moon. It hung there, delicate as the little gold crescent pin with tiny diamonds on it that my grandmother wore as long as she lived. Grannie McClure, are you up there now? And do you know that – ?

OLIVER: It was like waking up in a new world, that spring. But thank God you were there, and I was, too –

NORMA: We had been so in –

ABBEY: – or even more so. And then, one evening, when the moon was almost full, we saw this –

HARRY: We saw it too –

NORMA: Yes. Down that block –

HARRY: That old house –

OLIVER: With a broken window –

HARRY: Forget that!

ABBEY. A big garage.

OLIVER: A lawn to mow –

HARRY: A tree for a swing ...

NORMA: But why in the world are we – ?

ABBEY: Why are they – ?

NORMA: We looked back and they were standing there long after we finally walked on ...

HARRY: We saw you looking back.

OLIVER: Is that where it really began?

HARRY: It was the tree.

OLIVER: He couldn't get over that tree.

HARRY: How that one big branch was so – Not too high, and good and strong.

OLIVER: "Perfect. For a swing." He talked about it all the way home. And all week. Of course, he meant perfect – for a swing – for a child.

(In this following section a lighting change could help to indicate that HARRY and OLIVER are alone.)

HARRY: If I had a child, how I would love it. Make it know how I love it. I would wrap it in such tenderness all the days of its life –

OLIVER: His life. Her life.

HARRY: My life.

OLIVER: Our life.

HARRY: A child is a child –

OLIVER: – is a person! Don't people know that? Don't they care?

HARRY: And each, so different –

OLIVER: – as we know.

HARRY: God knows we know.

OLIVER: We knew.

HARRY: And when we knew –

OLIVER: God knows how we needed that love –

HARRY: All that love –

OLIVER: All the more than before –

HARRY: To be wrapped in that tenderness –

OLIVER: Not to feel, not to be –

HARRY: Beyond the pale –

OLIVER: A pariah –

HARRY: Not to be laughed at, to want to hide –

OLIVER: Not to want to stay buried alive in a book ... Sometimes more dead than alive ...

HARRY: Wanting to be "chosen by", "voted for", "believed in –"

OLIVER: But knowing that all there was left was the waiting –

HARRY: The waiting to leave. And to leave all the things unsaid, or the things said *and* unsaid –

OLIVER: The sins of commission. And the sins of omission. A lifetime of things unsaid.

HARRY: Oh, God. If I had a child –

OLIVER: If we had a child – How we would love it – If love begets love –

HARRY: – we have so much love we need to share it out –

OLIVER: – and we would pay attention if he, if she cried out "Love me, love me for me –"

HARRY: "For who I am –"

OLIVER: "as I am –"

HARRY: If we had a child.

OLIVER: Ah, my looks. Your brains –

HARRY: But it could only be yours. Or mine ... Either would be all right ...

OLIVER: ... But suppose – Look, sometimes women who want to have a child don't want to know who the – So suppose we didn't know, either – ?

HARRY: If it was – ? Or – ? But it would be one of us?

OLIVER: Wouldn't that make it "ours"?

HARRY: Yes. I think it would, to me. To you?

OLIVER: As close to it as –

HARRY: Oh, to have someone of our own!

OLIVER: But there's something else.

HARRY: Yes. A house –

OLIVER: – and a tree for a swing, and –

HARRY: Oh!

HARRY & OLIVER: – a mother ...

(In the following section a lighting change could help to indicate that NORMA and ABBEY are alone.)

ABBEY: That same week Norma wrote in her journal:

NORMA: "What I miss most. Spring on the farm. Lambing, calving, new life, birth. The earth, the trees. A tree is –"

ABBEY: That tree ... The one he said was a tree for a swing. You know what he meant ... Say it! "What I miss most is a child."

NORMA: All right! ... But we have each other. A good life. So much more than we ever –

ABBEY: And so much for that!

NORMA: No! I only meant –

ABBEY: "What I miss most is a child." Well, I do, too.

Our nephews and nieces, birthday gifts, Christmas, tears and tissue paper, and sticky hugs and –

NORMA: Kiss Aunt Norma, dear!

ABBEY: And wave goodbye to Abbey! And then they get back on the plane and disappear ...

NORMA: Or we do ... At the right moment.

ABBEY: Before the little question marks in parentheses begin to pop up all over the neighborhood? ... It was only once ...

NORMA: I'm sorry. Even so, I guess I'm only human. A human woman ...

ABBEY: Human ... woman ... That doesn't even rhyme.

NORMA: An imperfect rhyme. That's me.

ABBEY: That's us.

NORMA: And so, here we are –

ABBEY: And two Wongs don't make a white. And I'm sorry.

NORMA: If it were only that simple! This Wong isn't capable of bearing a child, anyway.

ABBEY: I know that, but it doesn't mean –

NORMA: I just can't help wishing there could be someone who would be some part of me after – part of you – part of ... us –

ABBEY: – after it's all over and –

NORMA: You have your books, but –

ABBEY: That's different! Sure, I'm proud of them, but –

NORMA: They're not enough?

ABBEY: No!

NORMA: I thought it might be, for you. I thought you were lucky because you have those –

ABBEY: I suppose I am, but that's not at all the same thing.

NORMA: Oh.

ABBEY: And it's not ... us. So, look, if you really want to –

NORMA: I would only want to if – If it could be ours. Not just –

ABBEY: Ah, your patience and my, uh, energy, yes. Ours, right? Sure.

NORMA: Exactly ... But – ?

ABBEY: Well, there is –

NORMA: If there were a –

ABBEY: Do you only read textbooks? Why not a newspaper! I mean, suppose –

NORMA: Dear God! What are you thinking?

ABBEY: Just *suppose* –

NORMA: All right ...

ABBEY: One of us, the egg. You! The other, the womb.

NORMA: You?

ABBEY: Wouldn't that make it not just mine, not just yours – Oh, not technically, I know, but –

NORMA: But as close to it as – You're serious?

ABBEY: I am. If you are.

NORMA: Of course I am. But that's only half the –

ABBEY: The better half. Don't laugh.

NORMA: We'll think of something.

ABBEY: There are places –

NORMA: That seems so –

ABBEY: And there are people. A child does need –

ABBEY & NORMA: – a father.

NORMA: "Our Father, who art in – ?"

ABBEY: Pray. Yes, do pray ...

*(Lighting change to indicate HARRY, OLIVER, NORMA and
ABBEY are together again.)*

OLIVER: The next week we walked there again.
HARRY: Down that block –
NORMA: That old house –
OLIVER: With a broken window –
HARRY: *(pointing to OLIVER)* Like a broken record –
ABBEY: A big garage –
OLIVER: A lawn to –
HARRY: A tree for a swing.
NORMA: Here we were –
OLIVER: "Together again!"
HARRY: ... Family house –
OLIVER: Bad investment –
NORMA: Dormer windows –
ABBEY: A fireplace – big chimney –
HARRY: Great place, huh?
ABBEY: Like you say –
HARRY: Great for a kid –
NORMA: If we had a kid –
HARRY: If you had a kid –
OLIVER: If who had a kid?
HARRY: If we had a kid –
OLIVER: Hey! Who's on second? Just kidding!
NORMA: Wish we were –
HARRY: What?
OLIVER: On second?
NORMA: No. Just kidding ...
OLIVER: Meaning?
NORMA: A kid, a kid would be great!

HARRY: Yeah, a kid of your own –
ABBEY: Yeah, that's what we meant, having a kid of our own.
HARRY: Your own –
ABBEY: Our own, yeah.
HARRY: Yeah. Our own. A kid of our own.
OLIVER: You're kidding ...
ABBEY: Down that block –
HARRY: That old house –
NORMA: And a tree for a – Were you kidding?
HARRY: Were you?
ABBEY: No. Not really.
NORMA: Not really at all.
OLIVER: Kidding or not, there really isn't an issue here, is there?
ABBEY: Nor will there ever be any issue, if –
HARRY: More's the pity –
OLIVER: The price you pay –
NORMA: For being. For being what I am –
ABBEY: For being what we are –
HARRY: What we are –
OLIVER: Yes, more's the pity.
HARRY: Damn, damn, damn ...
NORMA: As it was in the beginning –
ABBEY: Is now –
HARRY: And ever shall be –
NORMA: World without ... children –
OLIVER: Amen.
ABBEY: No!
OLIVER: So! ... All right. "Knock-knock."
ABBEY: "Who's there?"

NORMA: "Nobody ..."

HARRY: "Nobody who?"

OLIVER: "Nobody who gives a damn enough to want to talk about it."

ABBEY: All kidding aside? He's right.

NORMA: Yes. In the beginning was the word.

HARRY: A kid ...

OLIVER: Or a swing?

NORMA: Maybe a swing for a kid?

ABBEY: Or a kid for a swing – Whatever –

HARRY: Look. Tomorrow. Here. Right here. Same time. Let's talk.

NORMA: Yes.

OLIVER: *(to ABBEY)* And all kidding aside, whoever you are.

ABBEY: Abbey.

OLIVER: As in Abigail?

ABBEY: Tell you tomorrow, whoever you are.

NORMA: Down that block – That old house –

ABBEY: They were there first.

NORMA: Why did it feel like – coming home?

ABBEY: Hi!

OLIVER: Hey! You brought – ?

ABBEY: Lemonade. Look, do you think we could – ?

HARRY: The gate isn't locked.

NORMA: Actually it's ajar.

OLIVER: When is a – ? There's a joke –

NORMA: But – Wasn't it about a door, not a gate?

HARRY: Let's sit here –

OLIVER: Under your tree? ... Our tree?

HARRY: Under *the* tree.

*(A lighting change could indicate this brief interior thoughts
    section.)*
(To be played almost like a freeze, through "lemonade".)

HARRY: *(cont.) (to HIMSELF)* Is it just the tree? Is that
what this is all about?
OLIVER: *(to HIMSELF)* Is it just the old house, with that
– ?
ABBEY: *(to HERSELF)* Is it just this spring, this
incredible – ?
NORMA: *(to HERSELF)* Is it just as simple as the clock
ticking away?
OLIVER: Maybe a combination of –
NORMA: A culmination –
ABBEY: A confabulation –
HARRY: – over lemonade –

(Light change to indicate end of interior thought section.)
(As if "awaking" HARRY.)

HARRY: *(cont.)* Should I call the meeting to order? *(ALL
nod)* The subject seems to be: A child –
NORMA: – of our own.
HARRY: And, somehow, this house seems to have –
ABBEY: Become a part of –
OLIVER: The context for –
HARRY: So, the subject really seems to be – if I read this
right – A child of our own –
ABBEY: In a house of our own.
NORMA: Not a commune, no!
HARRY: *(pushes hand opposite directions)* I'd see it
more as his and hers –

NORMA: Yes.

OLIVER: Agreed. But do we send someone around to the real estate office first, or do we take up the other problem first?

NORMA: The child of our own. Look, the two of us have a plan and –

HARRY: And so do we.

ABBEY: Good. Then let's talk about that first –

OLIVER: Please! I think we ought to talk about us first, before we –

NORMA: He's right.

OLIVER: Couple by couple, we should –

ABBEY: Face the music –

OLIVER: And dance – actually, to continue dancing the dance we had already begun –

HARRY: The pavane –

NORMA: A court dance –

ABBEY: By couples –

HARRY: Slow and stately –

OLIVER: By and large –

ABBEY: But each couple must – ?

NORMA: Each couple. Yes.

OLIVER: Well! Abby?

ABBEY: Not as in Abigail. A-B-B-E-Y. As in Westminster.

HARRY: Aah! Gothic church where English monarchs crowned, and buried – along with a lot of other high mucky-mucks –

ABBEY: – and famous writers. They met there.

NORMA: Her parents. One summer.

ABBEY: Two tour groups colliding –

OLIVER: At half-past Alfred, Lord Tennyson?

ABBEY: It was Robert Browning, since you ask.

OLIVER: But collided with enduring effect? Lasting results?

ABBEY: Yes. Until it didn't –

OLIVER: Last?

ABBEY: Divorced, in the state of Connecticut ... And I'm a place name, not a people name ...

NORMA: You're a person and a place – And a whole world, to me –

OLIVER: But what a romantic meeting! *(to HARRY)* I wish we had met at –

ABBEY: – at my place, honey?

HARRY: Yes.

ABBEY: I wouldn't have been there – I never –

HARRY: You never – ?

ABBEY: Didn't want to, after the –

NORMA: I wanted her to go, with me –

OLIVER: You should –

ABBEY: I guess I could, now. Someday –

NORMA: Good.

OLIVER: Couldn't have been all that bad if there was you –

NORMA: – and a brother. Barney –

ABBEY: He's okay. For L.A. He likes you.

NORMA: What can he do?

HARRY: *Not* like you.

ABBEY: Like my mother. She tries ...

NORMA: God knows she tries!

ABBEY: But it always comes out wrong. If she could just – let it be.

NORMA: Let you be. Let us be. Like your dad –

ABBEY: Mister Show Biz – who never calls – But she picks up the phone in Greenwich – drinks her grapefruit juice – and grinds her teeth – over the grandmother thing! – As if she hadn't noticed that I – that we – Barney has twins – "But that's the son, not the daughter –" Is it my responsibility to her to – to –

OLIVER: No, Abbey, it isn't. It's not, not –

NORMA: Not her life.

HARRY: It is your life.

NORMA: Go on, say it. "This is my life!"

ABBEY: "And I'm not coming home to pick out my silver and –" Not that I don't wish I –

NORMA: That we don't wish –

ABBEY: We had someone to –

NORMA: Some way to –

ABBEY: But what about you? What's your –

OLIVER: Oliver ... And I'm just wild about Harry – and he's just wild about me –

HARRY: Aaaw. Just a song at twilight. He gets a whole musical.

OLIVER: With a twist, yeah! ... I grew up in Jersey – in the Oranges –

HARRY: And I grew up in the lemons, in Florida. Lemons! Ha! My grandfather had an Edsel. My father had me!

OLIVER: Hey, guy ... Besides, there's Jack Lemmon. He's okay too!

HARRY: Especially in "Some Like it ..."

OLIVER: ... There was "The Love for Three Oranges" – East Orange was not one of them. There was no love lost there – Not in my book –

HARRY: Missal –

OLIVER: Catholic school –

HARRY: *(pointing to OLIVER)* Guided missile –

OLIVER: Absolutely. By the collar. By the nape of the neck. By the seat of the pants.

HARRY: *(again referring to OLIVER)* Altar boy. First class Scout ... Not me. Wild kid. Loner. Blue collar.

OLIVER: Pale blue.

HARRY: Baby blue. School color. And a blue tie, too. Band concerts. Marching band. I did love that big old plastic tuba. Full of spit and mosquitoes ... Tons of –

OLIVER: Nuns, purgatory, confession, "Forgive me, Father, for I have –" penance, brass polish, floor wax. The cold ...

HARRY: The heat. Tent meetings. Holy Rollers. Preachers talking hellfire and damnation, warm beer, sweat, second-hand Harley. Highway patrol, cops, police stations –

OLIVER: Stations of the cross, Hail Marys, and hail to the Rose Mary who lent me books during that everlasting Lent ... Mary's month, and my mother, with her roses, with her rose-colored crystal rosary ...

HARRY: Rows and rows of pole beans – Rowing the river – "Across the River and into the Trees –" "Shall We Gather at the River" – and watch the gathering of the Klan ... ?

OLIVER: Don't get started on that! Harry's folks, a real estate office – One sister married – One unmarried –

HARRY: Was married – Oliver's father – Retired mail carrier – His mother –

OLIVER: Teacher – *Still* teaching – New dogs, old tricks – Always new dogs – !

HARRY: Oliver's two married brothers, that gang of kids – The Mafia – With freckles –

OLIVER: So. I fled the Oranges. Not with gun, but with camera – And Harry got himself up here – Out of the great gray green greasy Okefenokee – a six-pack or so later –

HARRY: ... A six-pack of scholarships ... A teacher – junior year – pointing out – "Thought you ought to know –" "Man to man", he said – "Your head maybe could be good for somethin' else besides – just backstoppin' that big mouth –"

OLIVER: – and a tuba.

HARRY: Yeah. *(to NORMA)* And what about you?

NORMA: But I already –

HARRY: You only talked about Abbey. Not yourself.

ABBEY: Norma?

NORMA: Minnesota –

ABBEY: A farm.

NORMA: And six brothers, yes. But I wasn't just a tomboy –

ABBEY: Despite the hair ribbons, ruffled dresses, Mary Janes, Barbie doll, the Easter bonnets –

NORMA: She loves those pictures – But talk about – disappointing your mother. Imagine how mine would have felt – But she died when I was only – Or maybe she did know – She told me – over and over – Be who you are, Norma. "To thine own self be –" I am, Ma!

HARRY: Six brothers ...

NORMA: Five now. Scattered all over the mid-West – Reunions at the lake – Decoration Day, Labor Day. Daddy, a little teary, on the porch now, wondering at what he hath wrought as the grandchildren pile up around him like puppies. Wondering if I'm okay – Back here, back East. Yes,

Daddy. Wondering about my life – About my ... friend – Wondering if it was something he did – or didn't do. No, Daddy. And, suddenly, this year, wondering where Ma was. Did I know? Had she been with me? Sometimes I wonder, too ... Maybe she has been. And sometimes with him, too ... At least, I hope so –

OLIVER: – so beautiful ...

ABBEY: I listen to her – and I wonder – Why does she claim she can only write how-to articles? You know, how to – screw it, glue it, do it?

HARRY: I don't believe it. I'm a photographer. Free-lance. How about you, Abbey?

NORMA: Her first novel's coming out soon – And she's had four children's books published. They're ... edible!

HARRY: I'm jealous. I edit a sort of weird trade magazine ...

OLIVER: Well ... somebody has to do it ... Or we run the risk of losing an incredible – albeit inedible – subculture – Vroom! Vroom!

HARRY: Racing cars. And I don't even care that much about driving –

OLIVER: Since the old Harley gave out.

HARRY: Okay. Show and tell is over –

OLIVER: And we're not Dick and Jane –

NORMA: Or Ozzie and Harriet –

HARRY: Or Mom and Pop –

ABBEY: Oh, stop! Not mine –

HARRY: We began to talk about the logistics and things gradually began to fall into place, but, even so, we went on talking things out, over and over, for days and days –

NORMA: – until we were about talked out. At least I thought so. But –

OLIVER: Yeah, but – Hey! Is it the inner child that demands the outer child? No offense, I'm just asking?

ABBEY: It's okay. Good question ... Meaning, do we deserve the outer child? But –

HARRY: Look! Maybe it's the inner adult that demands the outer child!

OLIVER: The inner adult? Oh! That poem of Robert Patrick's that he sent us!

ABBEY: Robert Patrick the playwright?

OLIVER: Yes.

ABBEY: The one who wrote –

NORMA: The inner adult. I like it. It sounds ... wonderful.

HARRY: Doesn't it! And why can't we have an inner adult instead of an inner child? Isn't it time?

OLIVER: High time!

ABBEY: Exactly!

NORMA: *(to HERSELF)* Time to stop just dreaming –

HARRY: *(to HIMSELF)* – this dream we never dared to dream before –

ABBEY: *(to HERSELF)* – this dream we thought beyond our dreams before –

OLIVER: *(to HIMSELF)* – now, if ever –

ABBEY: High time to be ... sentimental! To be celebratory!

HARRY: No. To be practical.

OLIVER: A friend works at a clinic where –

NORMA: Give me her number.

OLIVER: His number. It's okay. He –

ABBEY: Just find it, okay?

NORMA: *(to HARRY)* You'll call the real estate office?

HARRY: Yes.
OLIVER: This whole place needs paint.
NORMA: Then we'll paint it.
ABBEY: An ark. That's what it reminds me of.
HARRY: The Ark it is. If it's —
NORMA: If we —
ABBEY: If they —
OLIVER: If a lot of ifs ...
NORMA: But now the dream had become hope —
OLIVER: Hope had become courage —
ABBEY: And courage had taken hold —
HARRY: Under the tree —
NORMA: For a swing ... for a child ...
HARRY: A child. A prayer for a child, for —
NORMA: A gift, this life from life —
OLIVER: From life to life —
ABBEY: Pray for a child, our own child —
HARRY: Or as close to it as ...
NORMA: And pray for us this gift —
ABBEY: That our lives, too —
OLIVER: Bear repeating.
NORMA: *(writing)* "A recipe". Old as night. New as morning. As simple as the sun. As complicated as the moon.
ABBEY: A womb.
NORMA: An egg.
HARRY & OLIVER: And sperm.
NORMA: How extraordinary is the ... ordinary. The germ of it a-borning. The genes, the chromosomes ...
ABBEY: Tests! AIDS tests!
OLIVER: Why me?
ABBEY: You, me — all of us!

NORMA: All of us in this together.

ABBEY: *(to OLIVER)* Fussbudget.

OLIVER: Have budget. Will fuss.

HARRY: Group expense.

NORMA: Share the expense.

OLIVER: Spare no expense!

ABBEY: Nothing that's important before we – Oh, but this should all be being done so ... so sweetly, softly –

HARRY: Softly? Hardly! It's a life we're talking about!

ABBEY: Shouting about!

NORMA: About time.

OLIVER: Yes, timing, calendars, thermometers, experts, credit cards, cash, currency –

HARRY: And don't forget the termite inspection, the title search, the broken porch stairs and the mortgage for The Ark! Of course it all costs money! Everything does!

ABBEY: Unless you were planning to take it with you, the government would get it anyway, Oliver.

OLIVER: Sorry. Jumpy, I guess.

NORMA: Prospective fathers need to be in good shape, too, or else their sperm might not be – *(as if pointing to book)* – right here!

ABBEY: So cool it. I'm the one that should be –

HARRY: We all are, Abbey. Don't blame Oliver –

ABBEY: I know ... Oh, God. It's almost tomorrow.

NORMA: The clinic –

OLIVER: Currently located at –

HARRY: We know –

ABBEY: The northwest corner of –

NORMA: Is it time –

OLIVER: Yes –

ABBEY: – to go?

NORMA: Take hands –

HARRY: Take heart –

NORMA: Take egg, womb –

OLIVER & HARRY: And sperm –

ABBEY: Take Lexington Avenue local to –

OLIVER: Take subway token –

NORMA: Token of our love –

HARRY: Token of my affection –

ABBEY: Hold my hand?

NORMA: Cross my heart –

HARRY: And hope to –

OLIVER: Get set. Go!

NORMA: Sign in –

ABBEY: Wait here.

HARRY: Wait there.

OLIVER: Unlike that old song about South of the Border and the mission bells ringing, our tomorrow *had* come. But it was only the first of a lot of tomorrows –

HARRY: How hard to explain –

NORMA: How long to convince –

ABBEY: How easy to see them –

OLIVER: – wince –

HARRY: – unconvinced. Listen! It's all right!

ABBEY: It's *our* right ... Or our wrong ...

NORMA: No guilt.

ABBEY: No ... Just fright.

NORMA: Just nerves. Not wrong or right.

OLIVER: Our right to belong –

HARRY: – to feel guilty, to feel frightened, to feel nervous –

NORMA: – like everyone else!

OLIVER: Playing God to plan a child. That is playing God, isn't it?

ABBEY: Oh, God. We don't mean to be ... playing God, do we? Or does everyone feel like they –

HARRY: Abbey, I don't think we mean to be – And please don't cry.

ABBEY: No.

OLIVER: ... If planning a child is playing God, didn't God ... play God ... ?

NORMA: Sign here? I did!

ABBEY: Just sign it again. Sign there –

HARRY: Look! Don't pay any attention to those people!

OLIVER: It's our money –

NORMA: – our right. And our child, please God –

HARRY: If not here, then –

NORMA: Then there'll be somewhere else. If it's a fight –

OLIVER: We'll fight!

ABBEY: I saw them laugh –

NORMA: Let them. We'll have the last one, if the –

ABBEY: If it –

HARRY: If our –

OLIVER: If we –

HARRY: – win –

ABBEY: Sign here –

OLIVER: Sign there –

NORMA: Sign out –

OLIVER: Wait ...

HARRY: Call in –

ABBEY: Not yet –

OLIVER: Wait ...
NORMA: Call back –
OLIVER: Not yet –
ABBEY: Call Tuesday – ... I can't ...
HARRY: Call.
ABBEY: This is – Everything is ... okay!
HARRY: Oh, God!

(He's crying.)

NORMA: What, Harry?
HARRY: ... My mother. Just thinking – How proud she'll be! First time in my life she'll have ... something to say about me ... she can shout from the rooftops –
NORMA: We were all –
OLIVER: Exultant!
ABBEY: Well, I was, and I wasn't, at first.
NORMA: She means in the mornings. That's normal.
ABBEY: But it was me, not you. I'm sorry ... I promised I wouldn't –
HARRY: And you haven't!
OLIVER: Hey, you're great!
ABBEY: Well, I will be, I guess ...
NORMA: We'll go shopping soon, okay?
ABBEY: And would you believe Oliver's taking up knitting?
NORMA: Supposed to be a surprise. He said he'd rather do that than read. Penelope Leach every night, like Harry does. Whatever happened to Dr. Spock, anyway?
ABBEY: That's still around, too. *(as if reading folder)* Hmnnnn ... This La Leche outfit looks like a bunch of tough cookies ... Or should I say tough titties ...

NORMA: Ouch!

ABBEY: Yeah ...

NORMA: Listen, when you go for the test –

ABBEY: – the amniocentesis? Yeah?

NORMA: – will they tell us, uh, tell you, whether it's a –

ABBEY: Only if you want to know.

NORMA: Do we?

HARRY: Do we want to know if it's a –

OLIVER: – or a – ? Nooooo.

HARRY: I agree. But maybe they –

OLIVER: No, they don't either.

HARRY: Good. Let's just do this the old-fashioned way –

OLIVER: – so to speak –

NORMA: But they told her anyway. Even though she said she –

ABBEY: It's a boy. Are you glad?

HARRY: Half and half. Look, I'm just glad it –

NORMA: He –

OLIVER: Yeah, he, he is good and healthy –

ABBEY: He is. They say. Hey! Our son! How does that sound?

NORMA: *(as if writing)* Christmas Eve: God willing, we are going to have both a house and a son within the next two months.

HARRY: And in that order, I trust. There's a lot to be done there. That kitchen –

ABBEY: And a nursery ... Are you really making a cradle, Harry?

HARRY: Man cannot live on Penelope Leach alone, Abbey. Yes, I am making one ... Until we can get into the house I need to do so something real for him.

ABBEY: Him. I'm beginning to hate that. Isn't he going to have a name? So far, he's been an it and a him. Even the house has a name.

NORMA: The Ark, yes.

OLIVER: Then why not Noah — And then the house could be —

NORMA: — Noah's Ark? Oh, Oliver, that is just so —

(She makes a face.)

ABBEY: *(excited)* So perfect, actually.

OLIVER: Look, Norma, I was only —

ABBEY: Oliver, you're a genius. N for Norma, O for Oliver, A for Abbey —

OLIVER: and H for Harry! Ha! Look, I really didn't —

HARRY: I like it!

NORMA: Do you think ... Noah will ... ?

ABBEY: He'll love it. He loves it already. It all ... fits, doesn't it — Down the block —

HARRY: That old house — Next year we'll decorate the trees by the front door —

ABBEY: Merry Christmas, Noah!

OLIVER: And Happy New Year!

HARRY: The closing was ten days later, and with the help of —

OLIVER: — if you'll pardon the expression —

HARRY: — an architect, we were making good headway by late February.

NORMA: And so was Noah.

ABBEY: How the trimesters fly when you're having fun! Oh, oh, owwww — Are you timing? That was an hour long, wasn't it?

OLIVER: At least. But it's not how long – It's how long in between the –

NORMA: Men! Your bag's ready.

OLIVER: I'll take it downstairs and warm up the –

NORMA: It was a white night ... Awaiting a newborn ...

HARRY: Snow ... With our newborn hope, we awaited being newborn ourselves –

OLIVER: – white-lipped, knuckles white with – fear –

NORMA: A white-curtained cubicle –

ABBEY: Tidal waves of pain –

NORMA: Push!

ABBEY: Slush-piles of Muzak flowing down white-tiled walls –

NORMA: Push again!

ABBEY: Sterile stirrups shining in the bright light – I am a turkey, trussed for roasting, I tell them –

NORMA: Trust me, the obstetrician laughs – Carbonara breath!

HARRY: White cardboard coffee cups crushed into a wastebasket already overflowing –

ABBEY: I'm trying!

NORMA: Once more!

OLIVER: And at 4:30 A.M. –

NORMA: On the twenty-eighth day of February –

HARRY: In the year of our Lord, 1992 –

(The year may be advanced to conform to time scheme of production.)

ABBEY: Our son was born. Hello, Noah.

HARRY: For unto us –

OLIVER: All four of us –

HARRY: A child is born –

NORMA: Do we call on silent angels to witness our joy,

OLIVER: we four forebears?

NORMA: Our tomorrow was born today.

HARRY: We were happy beyond belief.

OLIVER: Relieved beyond belief. A hard day's night, Abbey.

ABBEY: Yes, but – For all of you, too. Did you know they said –

NORMA: We know. You can't have another ...

ABBEY: Well, we only asked for one ... Look, I know it's all just biological, but he's a – a –

HARRY: A miracle!

ABBEY: Yes. Isn't he?

OLIVER: Miracle Number Two.

NORMA: *(nodding)* That there could be love –

ABBEY: Could be you –

NORMA: Could be me –

HARRY: *(to OLIVER)* That we met –

OLIVER: That we knew – That was Miracle Number One.

NORMA: On a morning turned gentle –

HARRY: – March came in like a lamb –

NORMA: – we took Noah –

OLIVER: – and Abbey –

NORMA: – home.

HARRY: We walked into The Ark – couple by couple –

ABBEY: Two mothers –

OLIVER: Two fathers –

HARRY: With our miracle –

ABBEY: The miracle that made us ... a family. His family.

HARRY: He looks like –

OLIVER: Well, those hands are ...

ABBEY: But his eyes could be –

NORMA: His mouth – Is it yours?

HARRY: ... like us? Or none of us?

ABBEY: He looks like –

OLIVER: – like Noah!

ABBEY: And here, safe in Noah's Ark –

OLIVER: He eats, he sleeps, he grins –

NORMA: He smiles, laughs –

ABBEY: – looks at us –

HARRY: He knows our voices –

OLIVER: – and looks around for us –

NORMA: Looks to us for –

HARRY: We are his world –

ABBEY: – and he is our world, and here, together, in Noah's Ark, we are all safe – He sees colors now, reaches, touches –

OLIVER: Blows bubbles –

NORMA: Tries to turn over –

HARRY: Splashes in the tub –

ABBEY: Noah, wet and glowing –

OLIVER: Noah, crawling, crowing –

HARRY: Noah standing, filled with wonder –

NORMA: A different view for him –

ABBEY: For us, too. It's all happening so fast –

OLIVER: Growing, growing, growing – Yes, too fast –

HARRY: Noah walking –

NORMA: Noah talking –

ABBEY: Noah singing –

HARRY: Noah swinging –

ABBEY: Noah's birthday – Grandparents and presents –

OLIVER: One candle –

NORMA: And then two – More presents, and –

OLIVER: More photographs of Noah, piles of photographs –

ABBEY: Whole albums ... And videotapes of –

HARRY: Noah marching toward three, half-way there when –

NORMA: It was a golden week in late September –

ABBEY: Leaves were falling on Noah's hair –

OLIVER: His eyelids –

NORMA: His hands –

ABBEY: The leaves were turning early and there was a brilliant canopy of color over Noah, singing and swinging in the afternoon sunshine – But the next day, Noah was –

HARRY: Sick. Noah, who was never sick.

NORMA: Suddenly – Noah's forehead, Noah's fever –

OLIVER: Noah coughing, gasping – Noah frightened –

ABBEY: The medicines, the nightmares, 911 –

NORMA: Noah's teddy bear, the ambulance –

HARRY: Sirens, ICU, monitors, doctors, nurses –

ABBEY: I see you, Noah –

OLIVER: But Noah doesn't –

NORMA: We see you, Noah –

OLIVER: Oh, God, please ... No!

ABBEY: They tried.

NORMA: Yes.

HARRY: They said ... they were sorry.

OLIVER: What?

HARRY: Sorry. They were sorry ...

NORMA: Outside, the leaves went on falling –

ABBEY: They filled the sandbox –

OLIVER: Covered the blue pail and shovel with red and gold –

HARRY: But Noah was –

NORMA: Noah's coffin –

ABBEY: So small –

OLIVER: A blanket of white rosebuds –

HARRY: Scalded by the salt of our tears –

ABBEY: Released the scent of –

NORMA: Not summer –

OLIVER: Sorrow.

HARRY: *(as if reading)* O Merciful Father, whose face the angels of thy little ones do always behold in heaven; Grant us stedfastly to believe that this thy child hath been taken into the safe keeping of thine eternal love; through Jesus Christ our Lord ...

NORMA: We "stedfastly" believed, but –

HARRY: But what did that matter? We wanted to know why?

ABBEY: Why, God? ... The white linen handkerchief from my mother's bag is old and reminds me of – It must have been my grandmother's ...

OLIVER: Why, God? Why Noah? *(as if reading)* ...oh, Lord, look on us as we stand in thy presence in the fullness of our sorrow.

HARRY: Amen ...

NORMA: We were comforted –

OLIVER: – with apples – with letters – with calls –

ABBEY: – with callers – with casseroles –

HARRY: – with kindness and caring –

NORMA: – by friends, by neighbors – by relatives –

ABBEY: – most of all, by other parents –

OLIVER: – their understanding –

HARRY: – not just sympathy, but empathy –

NORMA: The death of a child is every parent's loss –

OLIVER: They said that it ...

HARRY: ... it diminishes them, us, us all –

ABBEY: We didn't know. Then. John Donne was still –

HARRY: Lit. 101, only a – But we felt not so alone ...

OLIVER: Not so "to ourselves" –

NORMA: Learned that shared grief can help to –

HARRY: It was one thing about us that we never doubted they understood. That they were all in this together with us, at this terrible time –

ABBEY: And it helped.

NORMA: When nothing else could.

OLIVER: When winter came –

ABBEY: We were already frozen –

HARRY: And mute, but wanting to howl, to scream –

NORMA: To run the vast, empty, windswept tundra of –

ABBEY: The disbelief of our loss –

OLIVER: Our arms, our flesh, our bones ached with the memory of holding Noah –

NORMA: Ached with the visceral longing, the unrelenting hunger to hold him again –

HARRY: *(to OLIVER)* To hear him calling you –

ABBEY: *(to NORMA)* To see him running down the hall to you –

NORMA: *(to ABBEY)* To watch you touch his cheek, the nape of his neck –

OLIVER: *(to HARRY)* To listen to you reading to him at –

HARRY: "Now I lay me down to sleep
I pray the Lord my soul to –"
OLIVER: "And if I die before I –"
NORMA: We loved and lost –
ABBEY: Were loved –
HARRY: *(comforting OLIVER)* Are lost –
ABBEY: And so we wintered over, each of us, and came through somehow – *(to HARRY)* – with your help –
NORMA: *(to OLIVER)* Cried through, on your shoulder –
OLIVER: *(to NORMA)* Raged through, while you held me –
HARRY: *(to ABBEY)* Fought through –
ABBEY: – together –
HARRY: And now it is spring again.
NORMA: Another incredible spring –
OLIVER: Like that other spring –
ABBEY: When we first saw –
HARRY: Down the block –
OLIVER: The old house –
HARRY: With a tree –
NORMA: For a swing ...
HARRY: The anger is gone –
OLIVER: The troubling deaf heaven with –
ABBEY: True grief –
NORMA: Pure grief ... is soft –
ABBEY: ... like summer rain.
HARRY: Was it better to have loved and –
NORMA: Than never to have – ?
OLIVER: Can we say it now –
HARRY: – and mean it?

ABBEY: I think so. Yes.

NORMA: Noah was; therefore, he is ... Because he is part of us ...

HARRY: And we are different because of Noah. He gave us a life beyond our own lives ...

OLIVER: We are older, wiser, stronger – and more vulnerable ...

ABBEY: We have been more loved, and are more loving ...

NORMA: In this spring of new beginnings, if we are not cured, we are healed –

OLIVER: And can move on.

ABBEY: And we are moving on. We leave for Atlanta tomorrow. Norma will be doing a series of new books, and I'll go on with my writing there –

HARRY: In a week, Oliver and I leave for Australia. Both with contracts, for a years work in Sydney and wherever – After that, we'll see –

NORMA: So we leave –

ABBEY: – this empty ark –

NORMA: – as we came, couple by couple –

HARRY: The story is over –

OLIVER: The pavane is ended –

ABBEY: And the musicians are silent –

OLIVER: Waiting for a new tune to be called –

HARRY: ... This ark – It is once upon another time –

NORMA: And some other child –

OLIVER: Another spring –

ABBEY: Will sing –

HARRY: – in Noah's swing ...

THE END

COSTUME PLOT

HARRY: Blue jeans and a light shirt.

NORMA: Light pants and light shirt.

ABBEY: Loose flowing simple print or flowered dress.

OLIVER: Khaki trousers and dark shirt.

PROPERTY PLOT

Four matching easy-to-handle chairs.

THE ART OF DATING

by

Jeffery Scott Elwell

*For
Edwina,
my constant source of inspiration.*

THE ART OF DATING was originally presented January 28, 29 and 31, 1994, at the Mississippi State University's Lab Works '94. It was directed by the author and the cast was as follows:

CAROL . . . . Stacey Matthews
BOB . . . . Ty Phillips
WAITER . . . . Tristram Brown

THE ART OF DATING was subsequently presented for eight performances beginning on September 15, 1994 under the artistic direction of Alexa Kelly at Pulse Ensemble Theatre, Theatre Row, New York City. Beth Lincks was the director and the cast was as follows:

CAROL . . . . Denise Casey
BOB . . . . Henry LeBlanc
WAITER . . . . Andrew Douglas Roth

Dramaturg: Gary Garrison
Lighting Designer: Kevin Lock
Production Stage Manager: Deborah Lopez

ABOUT THE AUTHOR

Jeffery Scott Elwell is Director of Theatre and a Professor at Mississippi State University. He received his Ph.D. from Southern Illinois University in 1985. A member of the Dramatists Guild, his plays have been produced by professional theatres in Chicago, Los Angeles, Memphis, New Orleans, New York, and Roanoke, Virginia. He is the Chair for the Playwrights Program of the A.T.H.E., Chair of the SETC New Play Project, and PAC Chair for ACTF Region IV. Six of his plays (including *The Art of Dating*) were produced on Theatre Row in 1994 and 1995. Two of those, *Escape From Bondage* and *Being Frank*, are published by Palmetto Play Service.

CHARACTERS:

BOB: Mid-thirties, a relationship consultant

CAROL: Early-thirties, a relationship consultant

WAITER

TIME & PLACE:

The near future. A crowded upscale restaurant.

THE ART OF DATING

*(A crowded restaurant. A man, BOB, seated at a table. He has
obviously been waiting for at least several minutes. He is
looking at a menu as a woman, CAROL, arrives. She
stands near the entrance, surveying the restaurant. He
sees her and stands, waving to her. She sees him and
walks over.)*

CAROL: Bob?
BOB: Carol?

*(They shake hands, BOB gestures for CAROL to sit. She does.
Then he sits down.)*

CAROL: I've never been here before.
BOB: Good food. Nice atmosphere. Quiet.
CAROL: *(smiling)* So, should we get down to business?

(A WAITER comes to their table.)

WAITER: Can I get you anything to drink?
BOB: *(looking at CAROL)* Please.
CAROL: Okay. I'll have a ...
BOB: Evian.
CAROL: *(smiling)* The same.
WAITER: Thank you.

(Exits)

CAROL: I'm sorry, I thought you were going to order a drink.

BOB: I never drink while on business. We are going to conduct some business?

CAROL: Of course.

BOB: Good. My client is a little impatient.

CAROL: Is he?

BOB: Yes. And yours?

CAROL: Interested but ...

BOB: You know the type ... feigns disinterest at first ...

CAROL: You've done a lot of these?

BOB: Dozens. You?

CAROL: Oh, I've done a ...

BOB: Your first time?

CAROL: *(laughing)* Hardly ...

BOB: You don't have to lie. I won't take advantage of your inexperience.

CAROL: *(sharply)* Don't worry.

BOB: Hey, nothing to get huffy about.

CAROL: I am not huffy. Insulted, yes. Huffy, no.

BOB: I didn't intend to ...

CAROL: No, I'm sure you didn't. Or maybe you did. Maybe this is how you work. Your game plan.

BOB: *(laughing)* Game plan? I think we've gotten off on the wrong foot. Besides, we're not here to trade insults, we're here to make an arrangement. Right?

CAROL: I detest that word.

BOB: Arrangement?

CAROL: It makes it all sound so mechanical.

BOB: Well, it is, isn't it? It wasn't this way when people still met each other face to face ...

CAROL: But that was before ...

BOB: Everything. I know.

CAROL: I can't believe how people behaved then. Engaged in ...

BOB: Casual sex?

CAROL: That's it. Can you imagine?

BOB: Well ...

CAROL: How foolish!

BOB: In retrospect, yes. But just think. If people had been sensible, we wouldn't have our jobs.

CAROL: I guess you're right.

BOB: Because then my client, Theodore, wouldn't have any use for me.

CAROL: No, it's much better now. So much safer. So much more sensible. And more likely to work out to each person's satisfaction.

BOB: Exactly!

CAROL: All the details worked out in advance.

BOB: Yes, now I really think we should ...

(The WAITER re-enters carrying their drinks.)

WAITER: *(placing drinks on the table)* Here we are.

BOB: Thank you. *(the WAITER exits.)* Now, as I was ...

CAROL: Yes.

BOB: My client ...

CAROL: Theodore.

BOB: Yes ... Theodore. Anyway, my client is very interested in setting up an appointment with your client ...

CAROL: Alice.

BOB: Yes, Alice. He is very interested in ...

CAROL: What does he do?

BOB: Do?

CAROL: Occupation?

BOB: Oh, I thought you meant ...

CAROL: No, we can discuss that later if it's warranted. Alice ... I mean, my client ... would simply like to know what your client does for a living.

BOB: He's a pilot.

CAROL: Excuse me ... *(she pulls a miniature tape recorder from her bag)* ... do you mind?

BOB: No, of course not. Go right ahead.

CAROL: Would you mind repeating that?

BOB: About his occupation?

CAROL: Yes.

BOB: Sure. *(into microphone)* He's a pilot.

CAROL: Good. Private or commercial?

BOB: Private.

CAROL: Corporation or individual?

BOB: Corporation.

CAROL: Risky, isn't it?

BOB: Accidents?

CAROL: No, downsizing ... mergers ... layoffs ...

BOB: He's been with them thirteen years.

CAROL: Very risky. Misplaced sense of loyalty. Salary?

BOB: High five figures.

CAROL: How high?

BOB: Higher than average.

CAROL: Eighty ... Ninety?

BOB: Seventy.

CAROL: Oh.

BOB: Excellent benefits.

CAROL: Life insurance?

BOB: That's a bit premature, isn't it?

CAROL: My client is concerned about the long-term as well as the short-term.

BOB: Two hundred percent of annual salary.

CAROL: AD and D?

BOB: Half a million.

CAROL: Age?

BOB: Forty-six.

CAROL: Height?

BOB: Six one.

CAROL: Weight?

BOB: Two-oh-four.

CAROL: Hmm ...

BOB: What?

CAROL: That's a bit on the heavy side.

BOB: He has an athletic build. At the gym three times a week.

CAROL: Blood pressure?

BOB: One twenty-nine over eighty-four.

CAROL: Resting pulse?

BOB: Fifty-six.

CAROL: Runner?

BOB: Rower.

CAROL: Interesting. Body fat?

BOB: Sixteen percent.

CAROL: Cholesterol?

BOB: HDL or LDL?

CAROL: Both.

BOB: HDL fifty. LDL one-ten.
CAROL: Good. *(a beat)* Chest?
BOB: Forty-six.
CAROL: Waist?
BOB: Thirty-six.
CAROL: Uh ...
BOB: What?
CAROL: I hate this next question.
BOB: It becomes routine after the first few dozen times.
CAROL: It seems so superfluous.
BOB: Then don't ask.
CAROL: I have to ... Alice ... my client has a preference
for ...
BOB: Well?
CAROL: *(looking away)* Size?
BOB: Specifically or will a general category do?
CAROL: Whatever you're comfortable with.
BOB: Average to above-average.
CAROL: You're sure?
BOB: *(a bit exasperated)* I haven't personally verified ...
CAROL: I didn't mean to ...
BOB: I know. *(pause)* You have more questions?
CAROL: A few.
BOB: Okay.
CAROL: Partners?
BOB: Lifetime or since the last testing?
CAROL: Both.
BOB: Thirty-three and one.
CAROL: Thirty-three?
BOB: What can I say?
CAROL: That seems a bit excessive.

BOB: Maybe. But you have to remember, my client was single and monogamy wasn't popular at the time.

CAROL: ... and no problems have ever surfaced in the testing?

BOB: No.

CAROL: Nothing?

BOB: It's all documented. *(hands her a slim file)* Anything else?

CAROL: Are you hungry?

BOB: Excuse me?

CAROL: Food? Dinner? I don't know about you but I'm famished.

BOB: Are we through?

CAROL: For the moment.

(BOB looks at the recorder. CAROL smiles sheepishly and turns it off.)

BOB: Thank you.

CAROL: *(looking at menu)* You've eaten here before?

BOB: Dozens of times.

CAROL: What's good?

BOB: I always have the same thing.

CAROL: Always?

BOB: Everytime. The house club salad, lite thousand island dressing, and Evian.

CAROL: *(smiling)* Very healthy.

BOB: I try.

CAROL: How about the blackened catfish?

BOB: I really haven't heard anything.

CAROL: *(removing glasses)* I like hot things.

BOB: *(nodding)* Heartburn.
CAROL: Excuse me?
BOB: I get heartburn if I eat spicy foods.
CAROL: That's too bad.
BOB: It's no big deal ... I just avoid spicy things.
CAROL: *(laughing)* Is that how you deal with your problems? Avoidance?
BOB: I wouldn't call heartburn a problem.
CAROL: I wasn't talking about heartburn. I can't believe that you always order the same thing. Don't you ever take a walk on the wild side? Try something different? Dangerous?
BOB: Not really.
CAROL: What do you do for fun?
BOB: Fun?
CAROL: That's right. When you're not working.
BOB: Not much. Nothing exciting, I'm afraid.
CAROL: That's too bad. You should be bolder.
BOB: I'm satisfied with my life the way it is.
CAROL: Are you?
BOB: Yes.

(The WAITER enters.)

WAITER: Are you ready to order?
BOB: Yes. *(to CAROL)* You are, aren't you?
CAROL: Yes. *(to WAITER)* I'll have the blackened catfish with rice pilaf and bleu cheese dressing on my salad.
WAITER: Sir?
BOB: *(looking at CAROL)* I'll have the same ... except for the dressing. Make mine lite thousand island.
WAITER: Yes, sir.

(The WAITER picks up the menus and exits.)

CAROL: Well.
BOB: Surprised?
CAROL: Yes.
BOB: Good.
CAROL: Why the sudden change?
BOB: I was swayed ... *(removing his glasses)* By you.
CAROL: *(taken aback)* Oh ...
BOB: You're not like the others.
CAROL: Others?
BOB: Relationship consultants. You're different. More human. *(a beat)* More attractive.
CAROL: *(almost blushing)* Thank you. I think.
BOB: It's a compliment. Believe me.
CAROL: So ...
BOB: So, how about if I ask a few questions while we're waiting for our food?
CAROL: Sure, why not.
BOB: *(smiling)* I still work the old-fashioned way. *(pulling out a pen and pad)* Your client is 38, correct?
CAROL: Yes.
BOB: Hair?
CAROL: Blonde.
BOB: Natural?
CAROL: Bottle.
BOB: Eyes?
CAROL: Blue.
BOB: Contacts?
CAROL: No.
BOB: And yours?
CAROL: Excuse me?

BOB: Your eyes?
CAROL: Mine are natural.
BOB: Good. *(a beat)* Bust?
CAROL: My client's?
BOB: *(blushing)* Yes.
CAROL: 34.
BOB: Oh.
CAROL: A breast man?
BOB: Excuse me?
CAROL: Your client likes large breasts?
BOB: *(shrugs)* It depends.
CAROL: On?
BOB: On the person. Not all men like big-breasted women.
CAROL: No?
BOB: No.
CAROL: What about you?
BOB: What about me?
CAROL: Do you like big-breasted women?
BOB: On occasion.
CAROL: I see ...
BOB: But it really doesn't matter to me.
CAROL: No?
BOB: No. *(a beat)* Now, getting back to your client ...
CAROL: Alice.
BOB: Yes. Is Alice athletic?
CAROL: *(smiling)* Is this a polite way to ask how much she weighs?
BOB: Not at all. My client is very into exercise ... rowing ... weightlifting ... hiking ...
CAROL: Aerobics. Three times a week for an hour.

BOB: Hmm.
CAROL: Jazz-tap twice a week.
BOB: A dancer.
CAROL: Five years of formal ballet training.
BOB: She must have strong legs.
CAROL: Yes.
BOB: You dance?
CAROL: Me? No. Not really.
BOB: You have very nice legs.
CAROL: *(a bit embarrassed)* Thank you.
BOB: You're very attractive.
CAROL: *(smiling)* That's sweet of you to say ... now, about Alice ...
BOB: *(recovering)* Yes ... your client ... she ...
CAROL: Yes.
BOB: I'm sorry. I'm a bit distracted tonight.
CAROL: Oh?
BOB: I'm usually all business. But ...
CAROL: Yes?
BOB: This is going to sound completely unprofessional, but ...
CAROL: Yes?
BOB: Are you at all attracted to me?
CAROL: What?
BOB: Attracted to me? Do you find me interesting?
CAROL: Well, I ...
BOB: Because ...
CAROL: Yes?
BOB: Because I am tremendously attracted to you. This probably sounds like ... a pick up line ... *(CAROL nods)* But it's not ... I'm truly ... genuinely ... attracted to you. But if you don't find me interesting ... if you're not in the least bit ...

CAROL: I think you're very nice.
BOB: Ouch!
CAROL: I mean ...
BOB: *(holding up hand)* It's okay. No need to explain.
CAROL: No. Really ...
BOB: Yes?
CAROL: I ...
BOB: This isn't necessary ...

(CAROL reaches out and grabs his arm.)

CAROL: Listen to me ... please?
BOB: Okay.
CAROL: *(letting go of his arm)* You caught me by surprise. *(a beat)* I didn't plan on ... I never thought about ...
BOB: This?
CAROL: Yes. It's not something I expected.
BOB: I know. I'm sorry. I've put you in an awkward position. Perhaps we should get back to work?
CAROL: Yes.
BOB: Fine. Partners?
CAROL: None in the last year.
BOB: None?
CAROL: Alice has been into safe sex.
BOB: Safe sex?
CAROL: Yes. You know ...
BOB: Abstinence.
CAROL: Alice prefers the term abnegation.
BOB: Abnegation?
CAROL: Yes. You know, the voluntary putting aside of something desired or desirable.

BOB: Oh.
CAROL: Is there something wrong?
BOB: That's fairly drastic, isn't it?
CAROL: I don't know ...
BOB: Although I guess it's different for women.
CAROL: Different ... how?
BOB: Men, you see ... men ... they ...
CAROL: Find it difficult to deny themselves?
BOB: I wouldn't say that.
CAROL: What would you say?
BOB: Men and women look for different things in a relationship.
CAROL: Go on.
BOB: Well, would *you*?
CAROL: Would I what?
BOB: Choose abnegation?
CAROL: That's a very personal question. *(BOB stares at her for several long seconds)* As a matter of fact I would.
BOB: You *would* choose to remain ... ?
CAROL: I've chosen to abstain from ...
BOB: Oh. Well, I didn't mean to imp ... I mean there's nothing wrong with ...
CAROL: No. There isn't. And you?
BOB: Celibacy? *(a beat)* No ... uh, I uh ...
CAROL: You don't have to explain. Like I said, it's a very personal decision.
BOB: Yes.

(BOB nervously begins rearranging his place setting. CAROL watches, smiling.)

CAROL: Why?

BOB: Excuse me?

CAROL: You wonder why I chose to ...

BOB: Oh, no ... I, uh ...

CAROL: Come on now. Tell the truth.

BOB: Well, I ... I mean it is a ...

CAROL: Bold choice?

BOB: Yes.

CAROL: I got tired of men. *(BOB, taking a sip of his Evian, slightly chokes. CAROL notices his reaction)* Not like, "I'm tired of men, I think I'll try women." I just got tired of dealing with men ... their problems.

BOB: Problems?

CAROL: Insecurities. Hang-ups. Difficulties.

BOB: A bad relationship?

CAROL: Not "a bad relationship." Bad relationships. Period. Looking back, they were all doomed from the start.

BOB: All?

CAROL: Not that there were that many.

BOB: I didn't mean to imply ...

CAROL: Like you said, men and women are looking for different things.

BOB: Right.

CAROL: So, what is your client looking for?

BOB: A relationship ... companionship ... maybe love ...

CAROL: *(laughing)* Love? Does that still exist?

BOB: Of course. *(a beat)* What? Don't you believe in love?

CAROL: Believe in it? Yes. Expect it? No.

BOB: Is that why you ...

CAROL: Why I've chosen *abstinence*? Yes, that has something to do with it.

BOB: So, you've given up on ever finding ... having ... love?

CAROL: Let's just say I'm not holding my breath. *(a beat)* Now, is your client ready to make a commitment?

BOB: Well, I wouldn't presume to speak for ...

CAROL: In other words, no?

BOB: I think it would depend on ...

CAROL: Don't say it.

BOB: Don't say what?

CAROL: That it depends on the person.

BOB: And why not? I mean, you can't expect my client ... or anyone else for that matter ... to commit to somebody they haven't yet met?

CAROL: What you can't expect is for any man to make a commitment and keep it.

BOB: That's a very pessimistic view.

CAROL: Maybe. But I come by it honestly. *(a beat)* In my experience ...

BOB: So now we're talking about you?

CAROL: Yes. Is that a problem?

BOB: No ... but I thought we were talking about our clients ... Theodore and Alice.

CAROL: We were talking about commitment.

BOB: And you asked if Theodore was ready to make a commitment to ...

CAROL: Anyone.

BOB: And I ...

CAROL: Wouldn't presume to speak for Theodore?

BOB: That's right. *(a beat)* On the other hand, some men *are* capable of commitment.

CAROL: Oh?

BOB: Yes. Take me for example.

CAROL: You?

BOB: Yes.

CAROL: Go on.

BOB: I'm very capable of commitment.

CAROL: I see. Are we talking long-term commitment?

BOB: What would you consider long-term?

CAROL: Co-habitation ... marriage ... Have you made that kind of commitment?

BOB: Not yet.

CAROL: But you plan to?

BOB: I'd like to.

CAROL: What's stopping you?

BOB: I haven't asked her.

CAROL: And this woman ... does she want this?

BOB: I think so. But I'm not sure. I haven't talked to her about it.

CAROL: Well, you'll never find out unless you ask. If you're really serious.

BOB: Oh, I'm serious.

CAROL: Good for you. And this woman ...

BOB: Yes?

CAROL: She's very lucky.

BOB: You think so?

CAROL: Definitely.

BOB: Me too. So.

CAROL: Yes?

BOB: Can I call your representative?

CAROL: What?

BOB: Your relationship consultant? You have one?

CAROL: Me? No. I mean ... I haven't had the ... you were talking about me ... long-term commitment ... but we just met ...

BOB: Yes?
CAROL: And I ...
BOB: Described yourself as very lucky.
CAROL: But I didn't know ... I didn't think ...
BOB: That I was talking about you?
CAROL: Yes.
BOB: Does that mean you don't want our representatives to make an ... to discuss terms?
CAROL: No ...
BOB: Oh, I ...
CAROL: No, I mean I don't have a representative. I, uh ... I haven't needed one lately.
BOB: Oh.
CAROL: So ...
BOB: So, it's not a problem. *(takes out his card case)* Here, take my card.

(She hesitates but then reaches out for it. She gives him her card as the WAITER enters, carrying two salads.)

WAITER: Here we are ... bleu cheese ... *(placing the salad in front of CAROL)* and the lite thousand island ... *(placing the salad in front of BOB)* Can I get you anything else?
CAROL: No, thank you. I think we've got everything we need.

(The lights fade to black as she looks at BOB and the WAITER looks at both of them.)

THE END

COSTUME PLOT

BOB: Dark suit
    White shirt
    Tie
    Dark socks (matching suit)
    Dark dress shoes
    Handkerchief
    Gold watch
    Eyeglasses

CAROL: Red dress
    Pantyhose
    Black pumps
    Eyeglasses
    Gold earrings
    Gold necklace
    Gold watch
    Eyeglasses

WAITER: Black pants
    White shirt
    Black tie
    Black socks
    Black shoes

PROPERTY PLOT

Two Tables
Four to eight chairs
Two white tablecloths
Two white cloth napkins
Two sets of silverware
Two water goblets
Two salad plates (with salad)
Two menus
Serving tray

BOB: Briefcase and contents:
              Notepad
              Pen
              Documents
              Business card case
              Business cards

CAROL: Purse (large) and contents:
                Small tape recorder
                Pen
                Checklist
                Business card

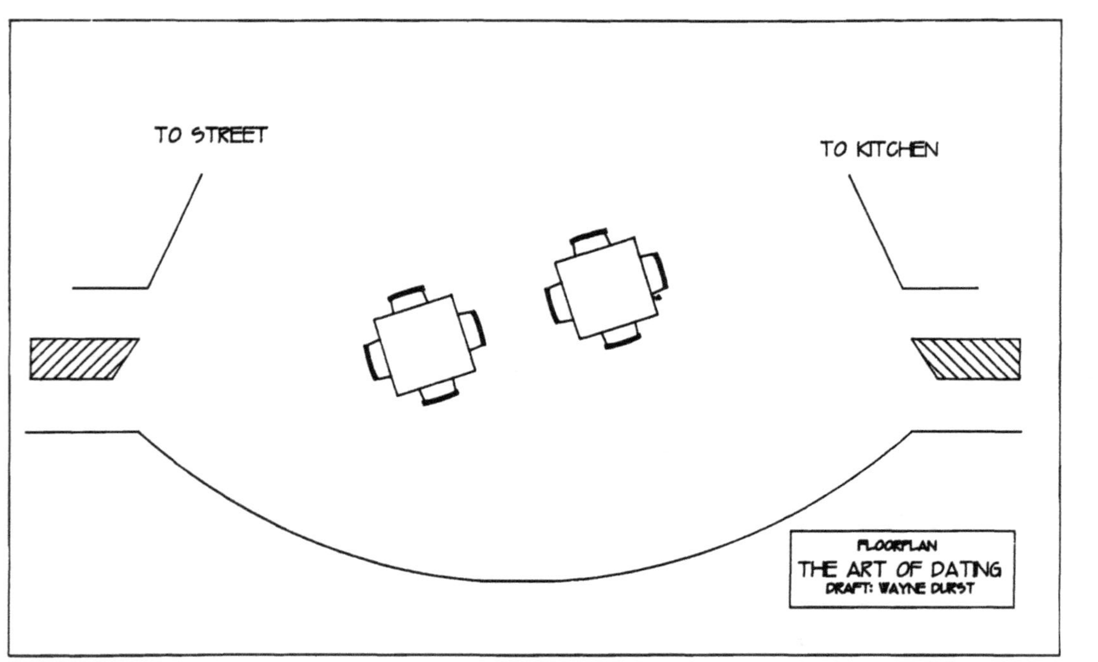

TO STREET
TO KITCHEN
FLOORPLAN
THE ART OF DATING
DRAFT: WAYNE DURST

SNOW STARS

A Very Short Play

by

Anne V. Sawyer

For Marcia

aspera ad astra

SNOW STARS was first performed at the Common Basis Theatre in New York City in April, 1994. It featured Marcia Haufrecht and Michael Sullivan and was directed by Lloyd Price.

ABOUT THE AUTHOR

Anne Sawyer was an actress for fifteen years before becoming a writer. She attended the Lee Strasberg Institute and later studied with Marcia Haufrecht, creative director of *Common Basis Theatre,* of which Anne is a founding member. *Common Basis* premiered Anne's first play, *Love Mud* and has continued to showcase her work, primarily one-act plays. *Meadow of Flowers* was a finalist in the 1993 Off-Off-Broadway Short Play Festival, and *Date Rape* was a winner of the Love Creek "Men in the 90's" Festival in 1994. Anne was a member of the Playwrights/Directors Unit of The Actors Studio from 1992 to 1994.

CHARACTERS:

GRACE: A woman.

CARL: A man.

SETTING:

Winter. Night. The sidewalk grating next to an office building.

SNOW STARS

(The stage is dark. Lights come up slowly, leaving pools of light which give the effect of streetlights on a sidewalk at night. GRACE enters, dragging a cart behind her which is loaded with items she will take out later. For now, she removes a plastic grocery crate and carefully places it against the wall, center stage. She arranges the cart next to her [SL], seats herself comfortably on the crate and takes an apple from her cart. She eats with a dainty but thorough hunger, gnawing the apple with machine-like precision and efficiency. Finally she pauses and resettles herself on the crate, then looks up at the sky.)

GRACE: Star light, star bright. *(pause)* So cold.

(She finishes the apple and pulls a coin purse from the cart and begins to count her change. CARL enters pushing a grocery cart loaded with cardboard.)

CARL: There you are.
GRACE: Mmm.
CARL: I thought maybe you'd be over at the bank building.
GRACE: Thought I gave you the slip. But you found me.
CARL: But then I was down there and I saw all those guys. Looked like they were up to no good. Those ash can fires are dangerous.

(He squats next to her over the grate, warming himself.)

GRACE: Warm, though.

CARL: Well, sure. They're warm. But dangerous. I seen a guy's head go up in flames once from one of those.

GRACE: You told me.

CARL: He ran around screaming. Looked like a match with feet.

GRACE: Stars are bright. Did you notice?

CARL: Huh? Oh, yeah. Anyway, we're gonna be snug as bugs tonight. *(CARL begins piecing cardboard together and building walls on either side of GRACE)* I was down by Safeway and found enough cardboard to build a mansion.

GRACE: Feels like snow.

CARL: I never understood how people can tell when it's going to snow. It just looks like winter to me.

GRACE: Look up. Between the clouds. See, there's one, there's another.

CARL: I don't see ... oh yeah. There's one.

GRACE: City lights are so bright we shouldn't even be able to see anything up there. Except maybe the moon. But we can. Because they're snow stars. Stars to wish on.

CARL: Wish away. I wish it was warmer. And they say the winters are getting milder. Global warming is gonna have 'em planting palm trees down the middle of Park Avenue. *(he laughs)* Maybe they'll turn the Lower East Side into beachfront property and put swimming pools on every block, too.

GRACE: It won't come soon enough for me.

CARL: Me either sweetheart. Can't you just feature it? You and me, wearing shorts, out on the Avenue E beach. We could get a couple of those lounge chairs. Maybe open a lemonade stand and make our money sitting down.

GRACE: Yeah. A ham sandwich in one hand and a beer in the other.

CARL: Yeah. *(posing)* Get your fresh lemonade here. Only two bucks a glass. Come on, you want to help me here?

GRACE: *(coughing hard)* Can't I rest a minute?

CARL: *(cowed)* Of course. I'm sorry. I just want to get this finished quick, so we can be on the inside, safe and warm. Then we can talk about stars and palm trees all you want. *(pause)* Are you okay?

GRACE: *(sniffling)* Yeah, I'm fine. Just cold.

CARL: Sure you are. Here. *(he puts his arm around her)* Better?

GRACE: S'okay. No luck at the shelter?

CARL: No. They were turning away folks with kids. Nobody wants to be out on a night like tonight.

GRACE: Don't I know it.

(She pulls blankets from cart and wraps them around herself.)

CARL: Yeah. God, I'm an idiot. I forgot. Some guy gave me five bucks. I didn't spend it yet. Figured you'd know better what we needed. He asked me why I was begging. I told him I had a big mortgage, bills from Christmas and all. He laughed. Maybe I could be a comedian. What do you think?

GRACE: Keep your day job.

CARL: *(a little hurt)* Well, first I'll get this built up so we've got a place to sleep, then I'll run get you a ham sandwich. What do you think of that?

GRACE: Ham.

CARL: Sure. There's an all-night place on Seventy-second Street. With a little spicy mustard and maybe a couple slices of provolone.

GRACE: I got some apples from over behind the supermarket.

CARL: I don't like you picking out of them bins.

GRACE: You want I should steal them? They're only bruised, anyway. Perfectly good.

(She bites an apple and hands it to him.)

CARL: *(he takes a bite, then spits)* Mush. *(he throws the apple)* Garbage.

GRACE: *(biting into a new apple)* Aw, shut up.

CARL: It doesn't matter, anyway. My gut's so cramped up I couldn't eat a fly.

GRACE: The day you eat flies, I'll eat your hat.

CARL: You'd get a stomachache for sure.

GRACE: Come here, you old fart.

CARL: Call me names, will you.

GRACE: I got a little something else for you.

CARL: Something to warm my bones?

GRACE: Maybe.

CARL: Something soft and sweet?

GRACE: With teeth to bite you.

CARL: Something to dream with?

GRACE: C'mere, sleeping beauty. *(pulls a bottle out of her cart)* I've been saving this.

CARL: *(swigs from the bottle)* Happy New Year. Ah.

GRACE: Well past by now.

*(She pulls a party horn or inflatable saxophone from her cart
and blows it up.)*

CARL: You should have come with me to see the year in.
GRACE: Aw, what for. I've seen it before.
CARL: I forgot. You've seen it all.
GRACE: Almost. When I was a little girl, bout three or
four, my daddy took me to Times Square to see them drop the
ball.
CARL: Aw, this again.
GRACE: Pretend you've never heard it before.
CARL: Alright. *(CARL takes the horn and pretends to
play it, humming the first few bars of Auld Lang Syne as
GRACE speaks)* He sat me up on his shoulders so I could see.
There were people everywhere. It was almost midnight and
we started counting down. Ten, nine, and the ball began to
gently fall ...
CARL & GRACE: eight, seven ...
GRACE: And when they got to six the ball stopped,
plunk, with a jerk, stuck, more than halfway up. So my father,
who was a sailor till he went color blind, shimmied up the
pole like a monkey and loosened the ball.
CARL: And he saved New Year's Eve that year.
GRACE: That's right, he did. And the wonder of it all
was ...
CARL: That when he shimmied up that pole he had you,
his baby girl, tucked inside his jacket like a little bird.
GRACE: And when the ball finally came down everyone
screamed and kissed and hugged and there I was, this bitty
bird girl in the middle of it all. High up in my daddy's arms.

(She drinks.)

CARL: What's going to happen to us?

GRACE: I don't know.

CARL: Can't you just see it? The palm trees. The sand. Lemonade, two bucks a glass.

GRACE: No.

CARL: Shit. Neither can I. We'll be okay.

GRACE: I don't think so.

CARL: I could try working that shoeshine stand again.

GRACE: You're too old.

CARL: I am not. Want me to go get that sandwich for you now?

GRACE: Just stay with me a while.

CARL: What was it like?

GRACE: What?

CARL: From the flagpole.

GRACE: Millions of people. You could feel them holding their breath. The faces, turned to us. Kind of shimmery like. Bright, like snow stars. Wishing for something new and special. Every one of them wishing for a miracle.

CARL: You're my miracle Grace.

GRACE: Shhh.

CARL: Everything will be okay.

GRACE: Sure it will.

CARL: Promise?

GRACE: Cross my heart.

(They huddle together, clothes wrapped around them until they are seemingly one. CARL pulls the cardboard flap closed.)

CARL: Happy New Year, Grace.

(Lights fade to black, a projection of falling snow.)

COSTUME PLOT

Both GRACE and CARL are dressed in layers of castoff clothes whose goal is to achieve warmth and whose fashionability is unimportant. A knit cap of some sort is essential for both, as are gloves, the fingers of which may be cut off. Additional clothes may be brought onstage in GRACE's cart.

PROPERTY LIST

GRACE: A wheeled shopping cart (containing:)
      A rectangular (plastic) milk crate for her to use as a seat, a blanket, two apples, a bottle of cheap vodka, a New Year's party favor or inflatable musical instrument, a coin purse with loose change, a pillow for the crate.

CARL: A wheeled cart, bungee cord, plastic shower curtain or drop cloth, large cardboard boxes, a five dollar bill.

SET NOTES: The wall in front of which GRACE sets up her cart should be no farther upstage than center. A flat may be used to represent the wall, or nothing but darkness behind the actors is sufficient. It is important only that they be not too far back from the audience.

LIFE COMES TO THE OLD MAID

by

Le Wilhelm

*Dedicated to all of us who have journeyed into the land of
Mave and to those of us who have once again found life.
To Nancy McDoniel and Irma St. Paule,
who were both wonderful as Mace in past productions.
As always, to Dr. Leslie Coger –
Southwest Missouri State University.
And especially to Philip Galbraith,
who directed both last year's Samuel French winner,
CHERRY BLEND WITH VANILLA, and this year's winner.*

LIFE COMES TO THE OLD MAID was originally presented by Love Creek at the Harold Clurman in 1994. The cast was as follows:

MAVE . . . . Diane Hoblit
FAY . . . . Wende O'Reilly

ABOUT THE AUTHOR

Mr. Wilhelm was born and raised in the Missouri Ozarks and attended Southwest Missouri State University and Florida State University. In New York City, Mr. Wilhelm is the Executive Artistic Director of Love Creek Productions, where he has produced and directed many acclaimed productions, including the World Premiere of *A Virgin Year* by D.L. Coburn (the Pulitzer Prize winning playwright of *The Gin Game*) and the Off-Broadway production of Bill Elverman's controversial crime drama, *The Mask*. In addition to producing and directing, Mr. Wilhelm is also an accomplished playwright and has won the Samuel French Short Play Festival and been published on five separate occasions. Mr. Wilhelm is also published in *Best Scenes of 1992, 1993 and 1994* and *Best Monologues for Women of 1992, 1993 and 1994*. His full length plays *Cucumbers, Pie Supper, One-Eyed Venus and the Brothers* and *Blackberry Frost* have been produced in the 1994-1995 season in Los Angeles, Missouri and Italy.

Other plays by Mr. Wilhelm published by Samuel French include *Strawberry Preserves, The Road to Niveah, The Power and the Glory* and *Cherry Blend with Vanilla*.

CHARACTERS:

MAVE: An old woman with a pronounced limp.

FAY: A young woman, in appearance could be a young Mave.

TIME & PLACE:

Anytime, Mave's home.

LIFE COMES TO THE OLD MAID

(MAVE us sitting at a table. She is reading the Bible. She is an old woman who has at one time or another badly broken her leg. She walks with a pronounced limp.)

MAVE: *(reading aloud softly)* The Lord is my shepherd. I shall not want. *(there is a knock)* He maketh me to lie down in green pastures. *(there is a knock, perhaps MAVE is frightened)* Yea, tho' I walk through the valley of the shadow of –

FAY: *(outside)* Open up. I know you're in there. Open up and let me in.

MAVE: You've got the wrong house. No one comes knocking at my door.

FAY: I do.

MAVE: I tell you, you got the wrong house.

FAY: No, I haven't, Mave McGinnis.

MAVE: How do you know my name?

FAY: I know a lot more than just your name, Mave.

MAVE: Who are you?

FAY: Some call me Fay.

MAVE: I don't know no Fays, so go on about your business.

FAY: I am at my business. I've come to visit you, Mave. I came to have a chat with you.

MAVE: I've no time for chatting.

FAY: You're lying, Mave McGinnis. You've got plenty

of time for a chat. Your Good Book tells you that you shouldn't be telling lies.

MAVE: I'm not lying. I've got things to do.

FAY: Like what?

MAVE: Got to weed the garden, got the dishes to do, got the house to dust –

FAY: There's plenty of time for that, Mave. Let me in.

MAVE: Who are you?

FAY: Someone who's come to pay you a visit.

MAVE: I don't want to be visited.

FAY: That's a mighty fine garden you have out back, Mave. I do believe you're got the best tomato plants in the whole county. Much better than Viola Jones', and Viola has nice tomato plants.

MAVE: Tomatoes did do well this year.

FAY: And the basil's so sweet, and the radishes – yes, Mave, I believe you have the prettiest garden I've ever seen.

MAVE: *(totally charmed)* Why, thank you.

FAY: Mave, I'm tired of standing out here. Let me come in and you can tell me what kind of magic you conjure up to have a garden like that.

MAVE: No magic. Just hard work.

FAY: Mave, let me in!!

MAVE: Are you death come to pay me a visit?

FAY: *(laughing)* Mave McGinnis!! I can assure you by all things holy I'm not death. Your Good Book tells you to do unto others –

MAVE: Alright, but I have the cleaning to do, and I have to give the garden a weeding. I can't spend too much time frittering away the day with idle chitchat.

(MAVE opens the door.)

FAY: *(at the door)* Thank you for asking me in.

MAVE: *(looking at her)* You remind me of someone. I'm not sure who.

FAY: Maybe it'll come to you.

MAVE: Would you like some tea?

FAY: If it isn't too much of a problem.

MAVE: No, I keep it brewed.

FAY: You have such beautiful flowers in your garden. The touch-me-nots are really splendid. They're my favorite.

MAVE: Mine, too.

FAY: *(smiling)* Yes.

MAVE: Here's the tea.

FAY: Thank you.

MAVE: Would you like a touch of honey to sweeten it a bit?

FAY: No, I drink it straight from the pot.

MAVE: Me, too.

FAY: This is delicious. I haven't tasted such good tea in ever so long. I haven't had tea like this since sitting in the living room of Rose McDowell.

MAVE: *(shocked)* Rose McDowell!!!?

FAY: You remember her, don't you?

MAVE: I remember her, but Rose died when I was a young woman. There's no way anyone as young as you could have had tea with Rose McDowell.

FAY: She always served it with a sprig of mint, even in the winter.

MAVE: *(afraid)* Who are you?

FAY: Fay. I'm a friend who's stopped to pay a visit on this late summer day.

MAVE: You seen so familiar.

FAY: Think on it, Mave. I'm sure you'll be remembering where you seen me before.

MAVE: You can't be staying long. I still got weeds to pull in the garden. I try to do a little every evening. Don't move like I once did. Broke my leg in a winter storm –

FAY: I imagine the weeds could do without a pulling just one summer evening.

MAVE: You go telling yourself that, 'fore you know it a week's gone by with no weeds pulled. Now what exactly did you want to chitchat about?

FAY: Whatever you'd like, Mave. How about when you were a girl? Remember the hay rides?

MAVE: *(without thinking of the fact that FAY couldn't know about this)* Oh, my yes.

FAY: And how we'd ride the hay wagons over to Barrel Springs and have a cookout.

MAVE: Wonderful fun!!

FAY: Hickory limbs always made the best campfires.

MAVE: You're right there. Hickory's the best – You couldn't have been there. That was nigh on to fifty years ago.

FAY: I was there, Mave. I remember it like yesterday. The hay rides, the fresh cider – and if it were around Halloween, the pumpkins with their ghoulish faces, Indian corn ... and the air – the air so nippy. I remember you had a bit of a shine, Mave. A bit of a shine for Theodore Bradford.

MAVE: *(this hurts)* Oh.

FAY: What's wrong, Mave?

MAVE: Nothing, but I have to get my garden weeded.

FAY: I do remember you and Teddy. He was handsome. I remember the dances, especially one dance. A fiddler came all the way from Chadwick. Fiddler Perkins. Remember Fiddler Perkins, Mave?

MAVE: I remember.

FAY: They had this big shindig back in a great room in an underground cave. And when Fiddler Perkins struck up the fiddle, I remember you and Teddy Bradford. I remember you two dancing a jig like no one had ever seen. I never seen anyone's feet move so fast before or since.

MAVE: When I was young, I liked dancing the jig.

FAY: You know, Mave, I believe that dance was even more impressive than that garden you got out back ... as a matter of fact, I know that jig was more impressive than the garden, and it is a mighty fine garden.

MAVE: I don't do the jig no more. But I do my best with the garden. You weren't with us back then. I know all of us. My mind is sound, and there wasn't anyone back then known as Fay.

FAY: You've forgotten me!

MAVE: No, I haven't. You weren't there.

FAY: Then how do I know all those things?

MAVE: I don't know. But what I'm beginning to suspect, I don't like.

FAY: I remember you and Teddy Bradford standing on the bank of the Little Blue River. I remember him telling you he was leaving, that he was going away, but that he'd send for you —

MAVE: No one was there.

FAY: But he did tell you he'd send for you.

MAVE: He told me that. But he didn't. And there wasn't no one but me and Teddy on the riverbank that day, and I never told anyone about his promise.

FAY: But I know that he gave you his promise.

MAVE: What are you?

FAY: Look at me, Mave. Remember back.

MAVE: You're a demon of some kind. Leave me alone!! Why do you want to torture me?

FAY: *(reaching out to comfort MAVE)* I'm not here to torture you.

MAVE: *(grabbing her bible)* Yea, though I walk through the valley of the shadow of –

MAVE & FAY: Death, I will fear no evil, for thou art with me.

MAVE: *(breaking off)* No demon can quote the holy scriptures.

FAY: I'm not a demon, Mave.

MAVE: You can't be evil if you touch the Bible and quote the scriptures.

FAY: I believe in the Good Book, Mave. I'm a might surprised you haven't recognized me by now. *(quietly)* Teddy Bradford shouldn't have made that promise to you. And when he broke it ... what did you do, Mave?

MAVE: You know so much, you tell me!

FAY: You locked yourself in this house and never had a thing to do with another human being.

MAVE: It's my life.

FAY: But it's been a lonely life for you, Mave McGinnis.

MAVE: It's been alright. You get used to not having people around. Got my garden, got my flowers ... and I got the hummingbirds that come to visit ... I got lots of things. And I've had about as much chatting as I can take for one day.

FAY: Fiddler Perkins was quite a jig player, wasn't he?

MAVE: He was good.

FAY: But there never was a fiddler that could play as splendid a jig as you was dancing that night in the cave. That dance you and Teddy Bradford was dancing, that was a sight. I can hear the music. *(slight soft sound of music)* Why don't you do a jig now, Mave?

MAVE: I can't dance with my leg the way it is.

FAY: You still don't know me, Mave?

MAVE: Just can't place you.

FAY: Go and get the album. The album where you keep all the pictures of when you was young.

MAVE: I haven't looked at that thing in years.

FAY: Not since you found out that Teddy had gone and got married. But get the album, Mave. I'm sure there's a picture or two of me in there.

MAVE: I'm not sure I know where it is.

FAY: It's in the top drawer of the dresser that's in the bedroom. But be careful, Mave. There's a dried corsage of yellow seven sister roses lying on top of it. They're a might fragile.

MAVE: If I get the album, will you leave?

FAY: If you want me to.

MAVE: I've got weeding that needs to be done.

FAY: Get the album.

(MAVE goes to get the album. She quickly returns.)

MAVE: Here it is. Have your look and then be gone.

FAY: *(looking)* This is a cute picture of you as a baby, Mave. *(MAVE doesn't look)* And here we are at the church picnic. And here's a picture of the hay wagon. And here I am standing with Teddy Bradford.

MAVE: There's no picture of you standing with Teddy Bradford in my album!!

FAY: Look and see.

MAVE: *(does so)* That's me when I was young. *(she sees that FAY is her young self)* Oh, my.

FAY: It's me, isn't it?

MAVE: Yes, but it's me. How can you be ... you're me when I was young.

FAY: When you danced the jig to the sound of Fiddler Perkin's fiddle.

MAVE: That's not possible.

FAY: I'm here.

MAVE: It's come my time, hasn't it? I'm going to die.

FAY: No, Mave. You're going to dance again.

MAVE: I can't dance. I told you I had an accident and broke my leg.

FAY: Doesn't matter. You and I are going to go dancing through fields of wild touch-me-nots, Mave.

MAVE: You're death, aren't you?

FAY: No, Mave. I'm life.

MAVE: Life?

FAY: It's time to live, Mave. Close your eyes and listen to the sound of the fiddle. I believe Fiddler Perkins is playing a fast one. You want to dance, don't you?

(We hear the music now, which will get louder until the end.)

MAVE: Yes.

FAY: Then close your eyes. That's right. Hear the music.

MAVE: I believe it's the tune that was playing that night.

FAY: I believe it is, Mave.

MAVE: I hope I haven't forgotten how to jig.

FAY: You haven't. It's like riding a bicycle. Hold my hand, Mave. We're going to dance like we've never danced. We're going to dance through the fields and on the streams. We're going to raise our dresses high and dance!

(The music is full and the two women, full of joy and a spirit of life, dance with abandon as the lights go to black.)

THE END

COSTUME PLOT

MAVE: An old housedress, decades out of fashion

FAY: Something flowering and diaphanous

PROPERTY PLOT '

An old photo album
Two teacups
Teapot
Bible

FLOOR PLAN

A table
Two chairs

THE APPOINTMENT

by

Luigi Jannuzzi

Dedicated with love to my wife,
Patricia Christensen Jannuzzi
and to my son,
Louis Christian Jannuzzi III

THE APPOINTMENT was first produced by Love Creek Productions on December 4th, 1994, at the Nat Horne Theatre, New York City. It was then restaged by Love Creek at the 20th Annual Off-Off Broadway Short Play Festival on May 16 & 21, 1995 with the same director and cast:

LARRY . . . . Stephen Shearer

TOEMEALI . . . . Alexander Lyras

GRACE . . . . Alysia Raycraft

MAGGIE LEWIS . . . . Gloria Vernick

Directed by: Lisa Mackie
Technical Coordinator: Richard Kent Green
Stage Manager: William Schwartz
Festival Coordinator: Geoffrey Tangeman
Artistic Director: Sharon Fallon
Literary Manager: Cynthia Granville
Executive Director: Le Wilhelm

Special Thanks: Waterfront Ensemble, Hoboken, NJ
Artistic Directors: Peter Ernst, Marc Duncan.
Double Image Theater: Helen Waren Mayer.
Sharon Schapow and Dr. William A. Stephany

ABOUT THE AUTHOR

The Appointment is Luigi Jannuzzi's third published play. It has been successful from classrooms to tournaments to the New York stage. *The Barbarians Are Coming,* Luigi Jannuzzi's second play, is also published by Samuel French. It has been successful from New York to Hollywood and also has won a Goshen Peace Prize. The author's first play, *A Bench at the Edge,* a co-winner of the Double Image Theater Festival, is published by Samuel French in *Off-Off-Broadway Festival Plays, Sixth series,* and has played from Hollywood to the Edinburgh Festival in Scotland.

Mr. Jannuzzi, born and raised in New Jersey, holds a B.A. in Philosophy and Theology from Salem College, W. VA. and a Masters Degree in Ethics from the University of Notre Dame. He is a member of the Dramatist Guild and a recipient of a 1987 New Jersey State Council of the Arts Fellowship and a 1995 National Endowment for the humanities.

CAST:
(In Order Of Appearance)

LARRY
TOEMEALI
GRACE
MAGGIE LEWIS

TIME:

7 Minutes to 3

PLACE:

A Waiting Room

THE APPOINTMENT
"I tried to make God smile and laugh,
God wouldn't.
I tried to make God angry,
God smiled and laughed."

L J

Note on language: If cursing is not permitted, tone it down.

THE APPOINTMENT

(Lights rise on LARRY at stage left, sitting at desk with phone, pen and book, reading a newspaper. At center are three chairs, and at stage right is a table with coffee, tea, sugar, milk, cups and doughnuts.)
(MR. TOEMEALI enters from stage right, looking around. TOEMEALI crosses to LARRY.)

TOEMEALI: Hi.

LARRY: *(looks up from newspaper)* Oh. Good afternoon. May I help you, Sir?

TOEMEALI: Yea. I got a three o'clock appointment with God.

LARRY: *(looking in book)* Three o'clock.

TOEMEALI: Yea.

LARRY: Uh, ... yes. Mr. William Tamelli?

TOEMEALI: Toemeali. Like *Toe Meal.*

LARRY: Sorry, Sir. Toemeali. Yes, you're on time, your appointment is at three o'clock.

(LARRY returns to reading paper. TOEMEALI stands there.)

TOEMEALI: Hey buddy?

LARRY: Yes?

TOEMEALI: Well, where the hell is he?

LARRY: You're going to have to watch your language, Sir.

TOEMEALI: Oh. *(laughs)* Sorry.

LARRY: That sort of language is not acceptable.

TOEMEALI: I'm sorry.

LARRY: In particular, this of all places is where you're going to have to control yourself.

TOEMEALI: Okay, I said I'm sorry, ... Jesus.

LARRY: Again you swear.

TOEMEALI: *(laughs)* Look, I'm nervous, I'm not too thrilled to be here.

LARRY: No one is thrilled.

TOEMEALI: I'm in business for myself. I don't have the time.

LARRY: No one is forcing you here.

TOEMEALI: I know no one's forcing me. I'm taking a chance if you know what I mean.

LARRY: I do.

TOEMEALI: But I'm lucky. I'll come out on top.

LARRY: I wish you the best, Sir. So take a seat, try to be patient. And there's coffee and doughnuts.

TOEMEALI: Naa, ... I don't drink that crap. Coffee's no good for you. Caffeine.

(TOEMEALI lights cigarette.)

LARRY: Mr. Toemeali, what did I just tell you?

TOEMEALI: I'm sorry. That's just the way I talk.

LARRY: Then we're going to have to stop talking that way.

TOEMEALI: Crap ain't a curse word.

LARRY: It's an unpleasant English word. And please put out the cigarette.

(TOEMEALI puts out cigarette.)

TOEMEALI: It's a dice game. *(laughs)* Ain't it?

LARRY: I hope you don't continue this line of talking with God.

TOEMEALI: Na. I got it figured out what I'm telling him.

LARRY: I would suggest honesty.

TOEMEALI: I'll be honest. Sure. But I figure you got to jazz it up a little.

(The phone rings.)

LARRY: *(answers phone)* Yes? *(to TOEMEALI)* Mr. Toemeali, it's five to three. Your appointment is at three. Have a seat, God will be with you in a moment.

TOEMEALI: All right.

LARRY: *(into phone)* Yes? *(TOEMEALI crosses to table, pours all the milk in a glass and drinks it) (into phone)* Okay, thank you. Bye.

TOEMEALI: Hey buddy?

LARRY: Yes?

TOEMEALI: How long do these appointments take?

LARRY: They vary.

TOEMEALI: But usually, how long?

LARRY: It depends on the person.

TOEMEALI: One of my friends, Reverend Albert Mays? Do you know him?

LARRY: Rev. Albert Mays, no I don't.

TOEMEALI: God should know him, huh?

LARRY: I hope so.

TOEMEALI: I hope so too. *(laughs)* He told me to come here, said it might help. I ain't got nothing to lose. So, I figure what the hell, huh? *(laughs)* Sorry. I figure, what the heck. I mean, does this help? People get help here?

LARRY: Some do.

TOEMEALI: I guess we'll see, huh?

(TOEMEALI begins pacing. GRACE enters from stage right, crosses past TOEMEALI.)

GRACE: Good afternoon.

TOEMEALI: Hi.

(GRACE walks up to desk.)

GRACE: Good afternoon.

LARRY: Afternoon.

GRACE: I believe I have a three o'clock appointment.

LARRY: Yes you do.

TOEMEALI: Excuse me. *(TOEMEALI walks up to desk)* Mrs. uh, ... excuse me. I couldn't help but overhear, you have a three o'clock appointment?

LARRY: That's correct.

TOEMEALI: She does?

LARRY: Yes.

TOEMEALI: How could she have a three o'clock, I do?

LARRY: She does.

TOEMEALI: Let me see the book.

LARRY: This is confidential information, Sir.

TOEMEALI: But how can she have an appointment if I have an appointment?

LARRY: You both have an appointment at three o'clock.

TOEMEALI: I don't understand. *(to GRACE)* Do you understand this? *(laughs, then to LARRY)* What's the story?

(GRACE crosses to the coffee table.)

LARRY: I'm sure God knows what's going on.

TOEMEALI: I hope somebody does. I just can't see how He can see two people at once.

LARRY: If you would just have a seat over there, God will be with you in a moment.

TOEMEALI: If you say so. *(GRACE is pouring water in cup. LARRY is reading paper. TOEMEALI opens wallet, takes out a ten dollar bill and folds it)* Uh, ... what is your name?

LARRY: Larry.

TOEMEALI: Larry, okay, ... uh look Larry, uh, ... I'm in a hurry. I mentioned that.

LARRY: Yes.

TOEMEALI: And uh, ... you know how everybody has friends they let go ahead? Well, if there's any possibility. *(TOEMEALI slips the ten on the book)* That's for the trouble.

LARRY: I do not accept ten dollar bills.

TOEMEALI: Shh. *(pause)* Okay, how's twenty?

LARRY: I don't accept bribes.

TOEMEALI: Shh, ... Jesus Christ.

LARRY: And I don't appreciate your language.

TOEMEALI: Look, you'll never see me again. What's the worry?

LARRY: I try to be fair.

TOEMEALI: So be a little fairer to me.

LARRY: Take your green piece of paper, have a seat.

GRACE: Larry, is there any more milk for coffee?

LARRY: I just put a new container out.

GRACE: It's empty.

LARRY: *(to TOEMEALI)* What'd you do, drink all the milk?

(LARRY rises from desk.)

TOEMEALI: Take the ten, buy more milk.

LARRY: I'll get another.

(LARRY exits upstage. GRACE crosses to center and sits in middle chair.)

GRACE: Bill, why'd you take so long to come here?

TOEMEALI: How'd you know my name?

GRACE: I saw it in the book. *(TOEMEALI reaches for book)* Wouldn't chance it if I were you. That's grounds for canceling your appointment.

TOEMEALI: And you'd be the first to tell, wouldn't you?

GRACE: Wouldn't even be caught with my hand on it.

(TOEMEALI takes his hand off.)

TOEMEALI: How come he let you see the book?

GRACE: Because I know Larry. I'm here often.

TOEMEALI: Yea, well look, ... your problem is your business, mine is my business.

GRACE: All right. I thought perhaps I could help.

TOEMEALI: You can help. Mind your own business.

GRACE: All right.

TOEMEALI: I don't understand this. My appointment's at three, it's five after three, he's five minutes late. What the hell's going on?

GRACE: You're going to have to watch your language, Mr. Toemeali.

TOEMEALI: Hey, don't tell me what to do. You got problems, work on them. I can take care of myself.

GRACE: All right.

TOEMEALI: I made my appointment at noon today, when'd you make yours?

GRACE: Around the same time.

TOEMEALI: But did you make it before or after noon?

GRACE: Exactly at noon.

TOEMEALI: Mine was *exactly* at noon.

(MAGGIE LEWIS enters from off stage right.)

MAGGIE: Excuse me, is this where God is?

GRACE: Yes.

TOEMEALI: He ain't showed up yet.

MAGGIE: Who would I see about an appointment?

GRACE: The fellow will be right back.

MAGGIE: Thank you.

(MAGGIE crossed to desk.)

TOEMEALI: If hers is at three, I'm leaving.

GRACE: That woman. Drank too much, went through a red light, caused a four car accident.

TOEMEALI: How do you know that?

GRACE: They're still working on her in the emergency room.

(LARRY enters with milk.)

LARRY: Hello.
MAGGIE: Hello.
GRACE: The same emergency room, they're working on you.
LARRY: I'll be right with you.

(LARRY walks over to table with milk.)

MAGGIE: All right.
TOEMEALI: How'd you know what hospital I'm in?
GRACE: Because I'm interested.
TOEMEALI: Because you're nosy, never mind interested.
LARRY: The milk's over there.
GRACE: Thank you, Larry.

(GRACE rises, walks to table.)

LARRY: And may I help you?
MAGGIE: I have an appointment to see God.
LARRY: Your name?
MAGGIE: Maggie Lewis.
LARRY: *(LARRY looks in his book)* Lewis.
MAGGIE: L-E-W-I-S.
LARRY: Yes. God is most anxious to see you, Maggie.
MAGGIE: I don't know if *I'm* so anxious.

LARRY: Your appointment is at three o'clock.

TOEMEALI: I don't believe it!

LARRY: So have a seat, God will be with you in a moment.

TOEMEALI: Wait a minute. Hold it. *(to GRACE)* Did you hear that?

GRACE: What?

TOEMEALI: Her appointment's at three o'clock. *(TOEMEALI crosses to desk)* Larry, Larry listen. How the hell can all these people have an appointment at three? And this is nothing against you Miss, this is a problem we've had before.

LARRY: Maggie, there's coffee, tea and some pastries. Help yourself.

MAGGIE: Thank you.

(MAGGIE crosses and sits in chair farthest stage right.)

TOEMEALI: What's going on, Larry?

LARRY: I am going to cancel your appointment if I hear one more foul word out of your mouth.

TOEMEALI: Larry, I don't understand what is going on.

(GRACE walks over and sits at center stage.)

GRACE: Hello.

MAGGIE: Hello.

TOEMEALI: Larry, look, I don't want these two listening to my problems.

GRACE: I'm sorry, Maggie.

LARRY: That's not up to me, Sir.

MAGGIE: I just can't believe it.

GRACE: Well, there's nothing more you can do but rest yourself.

TOEMEALI: And I'm not into group therapy if that's what this is. Larry, is that what this is, group therapy?

LARRY: Will you sit down over there and stop bothering me?

(TOEMEALI takes out small pad and pen.)

TOEMEALI: What's your last name Larry?

LARRY: Anngellino.

TOEMEALI: Larry Anngellino?

LARRY: That's right.

TOEMEALI: I'm going to mention your attitude, Larry. You're a bit snotty.

LARRY: Whatever you say.

TOEMEALI: Do you know it's ten after three?

LARRY: I do.

TOEMEALI: He's late. God's suppose to be responsible, ain't He? I mean, if He ain't, who is?

LARRY: If you would sit over there, Mr. Toemeali, the time would be more worthwhile.

TOEMEALI: What's that one's problem in the white shirt?

LARRY: I am not at liberty to discuss their problems.

TOEMEALI: The new one's in an accident. Did you know that? But I want to know the other one's problem.

LARRY: Maybe the other one doesn't have a problem.

TOEMEALI: She got problems, who would be here if they didn't?

LARRY: God.

TOEMEALI: *(laughs)* That's right, God. God would be here if He didn't have a problem, wouldn't He?

LARRY: *(rises)* I'll be right back, Mr. Toemeali.

MAGGIE: I just remember sitting there, starting the car.

(LARRY exits stage left.)

TOEMEALI: You know, maybe this is all a joke and all those ministers are just putting us on to come here?

GRACE: You believe that, Bill?

TOEMEALI: I believe it's twelve after three. *(TOEMEALI crosses to chair at left of GRACE)* But who said God was all-punctual. *(TOEMEALI sits down, leans forward)* So, you ran a red light?

MAGGIE: Excuse me?

TOEMEALI: I said, "You ran a red light?"

MAGGIE: Yes.

TOEMEALI: What do you want God to do about it?

MAGGIE: I don't know.

TOEMEALI: You're guilty.

MAGGIE: I know.

TOEMEALI: That's terrible.

MAGGIE: It is.

TOEMEALI: You're in big trouble kid. *(MAGGIE puts head in hands) (to GRACE)* And what's your problem?

GRACE: My problems, are the problems of others.

TOEMEALI: *(pause)* What are you on drugs?

GRACE: And perhaps I can help you, Bill. I know you hit a parked car while drinking.

TOEMEALI: First of all, I wasn't drinking. I had two drinks.

GRACE: And you're in critical condition.

TOEMEALI: Second, the car was double parked. So it's his liability. And I hope that's in the book there.

GRACE: So, may I help you, Bill? I'd like to.

TOEMEALI: Hey, that's okay, honey.

GRACE: I've helped others.

TOEMEALI: I think I'll wait for the big guy.

GRACE: It's up to you.

TOEMEALI: Yea, I think I'll wait.

GRACE: All right. *(pause)* Maggie, would you like to take a walk, I think maybe it may help.

TOEMEALI: Yea, take her with you.

GRACE: Maggie?

MAGGIE: I'd like to take a walk.

GRACE: Fine.

(GRACE and MAGGIE rise.)

TOEMEALI: Great.

MAGGIE: Thank you for asking.

GRACE: Let's take it slow.

MAGGIE: Okay.

(GRACE leads MAGGIE toward off left.)

GRACE: Why don't we go this way.

TOEMEALI: All right, two down, I'm next. *(TOEMEALI stands)* Now where's Larry?

(Before exiting GRACE turns.)

GRACE: Uh, ... Mr. Toemeali?

TOEMEALI: Oh God.

GRACE: Mr. Toemeali?

TOEMEALI: What?

GRACE: Would you like me to come back, perhaps you'd like to talk later?

TOEMEALI: That's quite all right.

GRACE: You're sure? I can stop by.

TOEMEALI: Hey, I'm positive!

GRACE: All right, Mr. Toemeali.

TOEMEALI: Ciao!

GRACE: I will though, Mr. Toemeali.

(GRACE exits stage left.)

TOEMEALI: *(to himself)* Get lost. They're both going down the tubes.

(LARRY enters from stage left and crosses to desk.)

LARRY: So Mr. Toemeali, how are you?

TOEMEALI: Well, I went through impatient and frustrated. I'm at vicious anger.

(LARRY folds newspaper, puts it in desk.)

LARRY: Your appointment didn't go well?

TOEMEALI: What appointment?

LARRY: Your appointment at three o'clock?

TOEMEALI: I never got it.

LARRY: Why not?

TOEMEALI: I don't know. He never showed up.

LARRY: Where were you at three o'clock?

TOEMEALI: I was right here.

LARRY: If you've been sitting here. Why didn't you see God?

TOEMEALI: I've just been sitting here listening to these two.

LARRY: Uh huh.

TOEMEALI: They were waiting too, but they took off. They just left. The lady in the white shirt is going to help the other lady.

LARRY: Did the lady in the white blouse offer to help you?

TOEMEALI: She wants to help everybody.

LARRY: I was afraid your appointment would go like this.

TOEMEALI: Now, do I get to see God or what?

LARRY: Your appointment is over, Mr. Toemeali.

TOEMEALI: My appointment's over? I haven't got it.

LARRY: Yes you have.

(LARRY picks up book.)

TOEMEALI: I knew it.

LARRY: And I'm leaving too.

TOEMEALI: I knew this was a rip off.

LARRY: You may eat the rest of the pastries and drink the rest of the milk.

TOEMEALI: Why don't you just admit there aren't appointments, or reasons for people to come here? Why put people on like this?

LARRY: You had your appointment, Mr. Toemeali.

TOEMEALI: Then how come I missed it?

LARRY: I don't know. I wasn't here.

TOEMEALI: Well I was.

LARRY: I'm sorry. I must be going.

TOEMEALI: Then can I sign up for another appointment?

LARRY: I'm sure it would go quite the same.

(LARRY begins to walk to stage left.)

TOEMEALI: Where're you going, Larry?

LARRY: I have work to do.

TOEMEALI: This is a big front. There's no appointments, ... only three chairs, a desk and a book.

LARRY: I think you didn't keep the appointment, not God.

TOEMEALI: I tell you, I was here, Larry.

LARRY: So was God, Mr. Toemeali.

TOEMEALI: I must have blinked and missed him. *(pause)* You know, I think I might be able to get out of this without Him anyway.

LARRY: Maybe you don't need anyone.

TOEMEALI: I usually don't.

LARRY: I'm shutting off the lights, Mr. Toemeali.

TOEMEALI: Oh great. What am I supposed to do, sit in the dark and wait?

LARRY: If you want to stay, you can, ... but you're going to have to do without light.

TOEMEALI: I'm gonna' be here for a while. I'm gonna wait a little longer.

LARRY: I'm sorry for the darkness. I'll be shutting them off as soon as I walk out.

TOEMEALI: Yea, thanks. *(LARRY exits stage left)* Great! Thanks Larry! *(TOEMEALI takes a cigarette lighter out of his pocket and lights it) (All lights go out except for the lighter)* Terrific. *(TOEMEALI moves to edge of stage)* What the hell am I supposed to do, sit in the dark and wait for God? *(TOEMEALI yells)* What the hell am I suppose to to sit in the dark? *(TOEMEALI yells)* Hey, what the hell am I supposed to do?

(The flame fades out.)

BLACKOUT

COSTUME PLOT

LARRY: Suit and tie
Overcoat
Conservative shoes

TOEMEALI: Sharp dresser
Well groomed
Stylish go-getter

GRACE: White blouse
Blue pants
Conservative shoes

MAGGIE LEWIS: Colored blouse
Nice shirt
Low heels
Stylish handbag

PERSONAL PROPS

TOEMEALI: Cigarettes
A lighter
Wallet with a $10 & $20 bill
Small note pad and pen

PROPERTY PLOT

STAGE LEFT: Chair
        Desk
        Phone
        Book
        Pen
        Tabloid newspaper that reads of current
          scandal

CENTER STAGE: Three chairs

STAGE RIGHT: Table
        Pot of tea
        Pot of coffee
        Sugar
        Small milk container and glass
        Doughnuts
        Cups
        Spoons

OFF STAGE LEFT: Another small milk container

Note on Symbolism:
  The 3 chairs could symbolize 3 crosses and represent
Jesus and two thieves during the crucifixion.

3 chairs
chair
DESK
phone
Book
+
Pen
+
Newspaper
Tea
Coffee
Sugar
milk
Doughnuts
Cups
Table

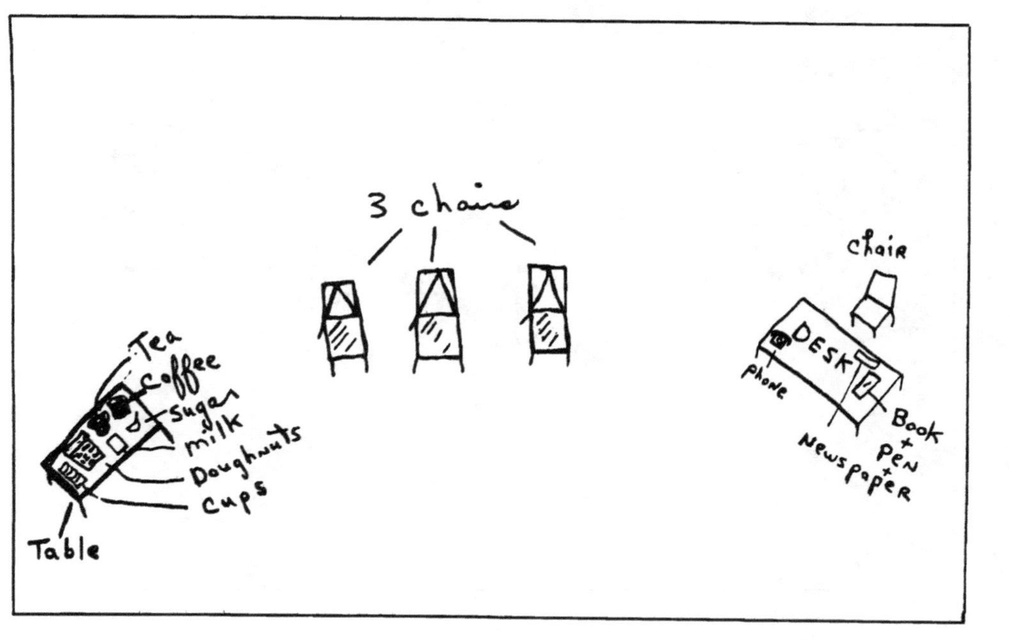

Audience

3 chairs
Tea
Coffee
Sugar
Milk
Doughnuts
Cups
Table
chair
DESK
phone
Book
+
Pen
+
Newspaper

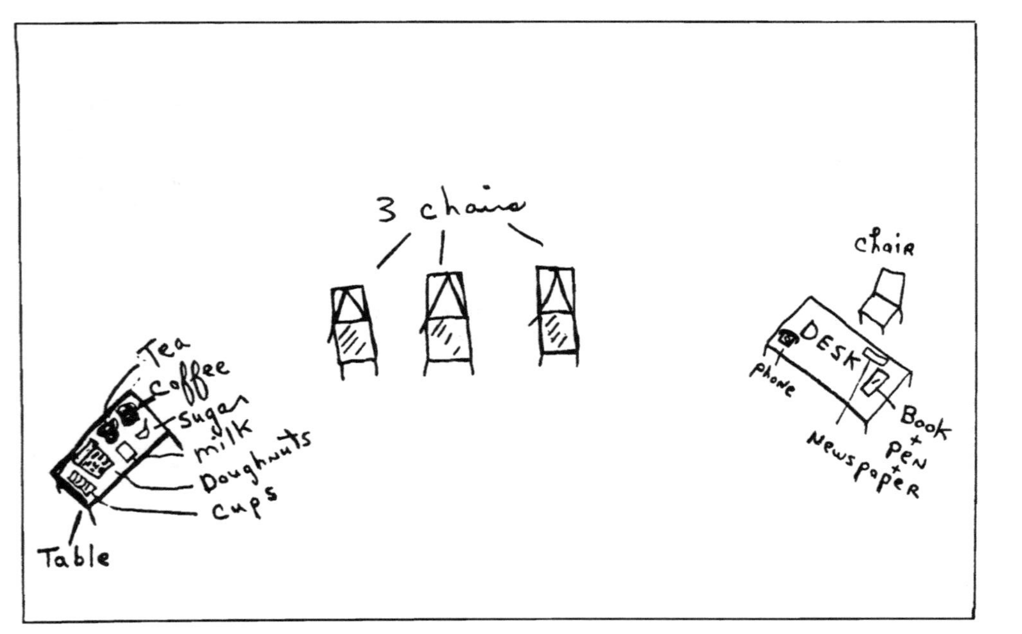

Audience

A WINTER REUNION

by

Henry Miller

*To my grandfather, John Fluellen, and one of his daughters,
my mother, the two people who, quite unknowingly,
gave me my first glimpse of the beauties of dramatic speech.*

After its development at *The James Baldwin Writers Workshop Theatre* in East Harlem, *A WINTER REUNION* was first produced on May 16, 1995 by *Theatre International, Inc.* as part of the SAMUEL FRENCH 20th ANNUAL OFF-OFF BROADWAY SHORT-PLAY FESTIVAL held at *The Harold Clurman Theatre,* 412 West 42nd Street in New York City. The cast and production staff were as follows:

BOB . . . . William Jay Marshall
JEFFREY . . . . Rudel Drears
LYDIA . . . . Rose Philip

Director: Henry Miller
Technical Direction & Set Design: Ajene D. Washington
Production Stg. Mgr.: Tara Gallagher
Production Assts.: Willi Wong & Tim Torres
Producers: Rey Allen & Henry Miller

Production rehearsal and location services were donated by THE RED CARPET THEATRE, TAINO TOWERS, Inc. 240 E. 123rd Street, NYC and MARJORIE ELIOT, PARLOUR ENTERTAINMENT, 555 Edgecombe Avenue, NYC.

ABOUT THE AUTHOR

Writer/Director Henry Miller, a veteran of the 1960s/70s African-American Theatre movement, is the founder and Artistic Director of *The James Baldwin Writers Workshop Theatre.* He has directed over 30 Off-Off-Broadway and regional theatre stage productions, and his half-hour film, *Death of a Dunbar Girl,* has been shown internationally and at the *Public Theatre* and *The Whitney Museum of American Art* in New York. Mr. Miller has written for *Columbia Pictures, Inc., The Afro-American Rep Theatre, The Afro-American Historical and Cultural Museum* in Philadelphia, and *The New York Village Voice.* He has studied playwriting under *Phillip Hayes Dean, Arthur Kopit,* and *John Guare.* He is also the recipient of the Magnet Fellowship for doctural studies in Theatre at New York's Graduate School and University Center (CUNY).

CHARACTERS

BOB: An elderly man, the Sexton of a church in Harlem, NY.

JEFFREY: Bob's grandson, 23, a postgraduate student at an Ivy League University.

LYDIA: Bob's only daughter, 45, Jeffrey's estranged mother.

A WINTER REUNION

Scene One

(A church rectory in Harlem, New York. Christmas Eve. The present, about forty minutes before midnight ...)

(BOB enters dressed in flannel pajamas and a terry-cloth robe. A small pillow is tucked under his arm. He carries a radio/cassette player and a book. He puts the book and player on a table by a fireplace and the pillow into the chair next to the table. He removes a tape from a pocket of his robe, pops it into the player. He pushes a button on the machine and moves to a nearby cabinet.)

(He liberates a glass and decanter from the cabinet as Nat King Cole's "Christmas Song" comes from the player. Contentedly, he sings or rather mumbles along with the tape as he sits down in the chair by the fire; he pours, he reads ...)

(Momentarily, there's a knocking and a muffled voice at an off stage foyer door:)

JEFFREY: *(off stage)* Grandpop? ... Grandpop ... ?

BOB: Huh ... ? Who's that? *(more knocking; he turns down the player)* Who's that?

JEFFREY: *(off stage) (comically)* And who is that?

(JEFFREY laughs; Bob pauses, then laughs.)

BOB: Fool ... *(he starts to the foyer)* Who dat, say who dat, when I say who dat?

(He exits. Off stage, a door opens; the two men laugh.)

BOB: Boy, what are you doin'? – get in here outa that weather ...

(The door closes; JEFFREY appears in the foyer doorway removing his coat. He's tallish, handsome, about 23; he has a scrubbed-clean look that sparkles with enthusiasm and intellect.)

JEFFREY: *(hanging his coat on a rack in the hall)* And what are you doin' in here with all this pretty Christmas music? All alone? Better check you out. *(he starts into the room)* Okay ladies. That's all. Got to go. The grandson has arrived unexpectedly.
BOB: *(delighted)* Young fool. What are you doin' here –
JEFFREY: *(moving to the table)* Ah ha, a good book and sherry by the hearth, too, I see. *(he looks at the book)* Hmm, "Before The Mayflower." Good. Getting your historical "roots" together, huh, Grandpop?
BOB: Now that's somethin' you oughta read.
JEFFREY: I did. You gave me a copy when I was fourteen. *(he picks up the decanter)* It appears I've arrived not a moment too soon.
BOB: So you into drinking now, too, huh?
JEFFREY: Too?
BOB: *(he laughs)* Answer my question?
JEFFREY: Only when I have traversed an arctic blizzard through the wilds of the ghet-toe to see my grandfather.

BOB: *(still delighted)* I see you still talkin' funny.

JEFFREY: What can I do? Over educated.

BOB: *(deeply moved)* Jeffrey ... look at you, boy.

JEFFREY: *(smiling broadly)* How've you been, Grandpop?

BOB: Good. How you been?

JEFFREY: I've been good.

BOB: Studyin'?

JEFFREY: Hard.

BOB: Hmm ... *(he goes to the cabinet to get another glass)* Guess they stop teachin' about that man by the name o' Alexander Gray-ham Bell. You, know, the one invented that thing with the numbers and buttons on it – Yeah, you actually can talk to people on it, at great distances.

JEFFREY: Now Grandpop, wait a min –

BOB: *(he moves to table, pours for JEFFREY)* You can even get in touch with old people on that thing. Can you beat that – guess they don't tell nobody about somethin' that insignificant when they up there studyin' for a Masters degree.

JEFFREY: Now, Grandpop. I called you.

BOB: Three months ago. And you didn't say nothin' 'bout showin' up here on Christmas Eve night, either. *(giving JEFFREY the drink)* There you go.

JEFFREY: I wanted to surprise you.

BOB: You wanted to scare me half to death, take me right on outa here before my time. You shoulda called.

JEFFREY: *(crosses to phone on the desk)* Oh, well, like they say: "better late than never."

BOB: Boy, what are you doing – ?

JEFFREY: Just a second. Won't take but a minute.

(He lifts the receiver.)

BOB: *(charmed, sitting down)* You are absolutely nuts, you know that? – get off that –

JEFFREY: Let's see. *(punching in the numbers)* 280-4173.

(He hangs up the receiver ...)

BOB: I always knew you weren't right-bright. How'd they let you into that university – ?

(The phone rings.)

JEFFREY: Zounds! A call at this hour of the night.

(He snatches up the receiver.)

BOB: Zounds? Now what kinda o' word is that for a young black man to use?

JEFFREY: *(into the phone)* Hello. I'd like to place a collect call to, uh, uh –

BOB: Collect. Uh hmm – I'm not paying you no mind, Jeffrey Townsend –

JEFFREY: Uh, oh, that's right, to Mr. Robert W. Townsend in Harlem – Okay I'll hold ...

BOB: *(pretending to read)* They oughta stop emptyin' out these mental institutions on Christmas Eve – Zounds – what kinda word is that? College-boy-ease that's what it is –

JEFFREY: *(into the phone)* Hello – what's that? *(to BOB)* Oh, I don't sound quite black enough to be placing this call. Sorry: *(again, into the phone)* Yo Bro. Hook me up to Bobby T in the village of Harlem, Right. Chill. Word. Dope. You know what I'm sayin', etcetera – Better?

BOB: *(laughing inspite of himself)* Fool, I toldya, I'm not paying you no mind.

JEFFREY: *(into the phone)* What? Is old Bobby T famous? Well, I know the dude pretty well ... No, m' man he ain't rich, either. Look, I don't want Strivers Row, I want 116th and Lenox. Right. Bring it on down funky. He's my Grandpop. You know, like father raised to the second power. Now y' got it, brother. Word Up! Huh? Yo, Bro, he's just a man – no, not The Man, a man.

BOB: Jeffrey, boy, if you don't get off that phone –

JEFFREY: A good man ... *(he lowers the receiver)* A very good man ... for me, he's the most important man in the world.

(BOB looks at him a moment.)

BOB: Crazy as a betsy bug. Now you tryin' to get somebody upset. That's what you up to ...

JEFFREY: *(smiling)* If I am, it's pretty hopeless, isn't it? Cheap sentiment could never get to a tough old bird like you, not even on Christmas Eve.

BOB: Y' got that right. Now sit down; tell me whatcha been doing with yourself.

(JEFFREY looks at him a moment.)

JEFFREY: Grandpop. I want you to do a little something for me.

BOB: Uh huh, see there, I knew all this butterin' up wasn't for nothin'. C'mon, sit down here by me.

(JEFFREY gets a metal folding chair, crosses to BOB.)

JEFFREY: You realize of course you're talking to me like I was still ten years old.

(He sits in the metal chair.)

BOB: Look, I know the year, month, day, hour and minute you were born. Wrote it down in my dictionary, Mister Big Shot. Now, whatcha need? Money?
JEFFREY: No ... And just why do you think I need money all the time?
BOB: Money makes the world go round, boy. I know you're kinda strange, but everybody needs money.
JEFFREY: Not from you I don't. Not every time you write. You know, the Post Office does deliver letters without checks in them.
BOB: Your Grandmama sends you money, don't she?
JEFFREY: What are you in competition with her?
BOB: I don't have to compete with nobody. I got one grandchild in this world and I mean to see that he's straight, that's all. Of course I guess what I send don't add up to what she can afford –
JEFFREY: Grandpop –
BOB: How's she doing, anyway?

(JEFFREY looks at him a moment.)

JEFFREY: She's fine ... Christmasing in the Bahamas.

BOB: More power to her. And that old man she married – what's his name again? Darknight, Allright, Benbright –

JEFFREY: Benjamin Wainwright. And I think you know he's only a few years older than you are.

BOB: Is he? Can you beat that. Man always looked so old. Guess it's that undertaker business. Work with the dead too long and you begin to look like one of 'em. Sure glad you didn't take up that field of endeavor.

(JEFFREY stands, moves to the desk.)

JEFFREY: Benjamin has sold the business.

BOB: Oh. Did he? You didn't tell me about that.

JEFFREY: I wasn't tryin' to hide it. The deal went through only about a month ago.

BOB: And now they celebratin' in the Bahamas. Well, like I said, more power to 'em.

JEFFREY: Look, Grandpop –

BOB: Guess your Grandmama really sending you them fat checks now, huh, boy?

JEFFREY: *(carefully and crossing to the fireplace)* Yeah ... Uh, Benjamin has set up little trust fund for me. I get it when I'm thirty.

(He puts his drink on the small table.)

BOB: Trust fund! Well, big time colored folks – and I *trust* that you will get it. Guess now you really don't need my little chicken-scratch.

JEFFREY: *(moving to BOB)* No. But I need you, old man.

(BOB looks at him a moment.)

BOB: Sure, Jeffrey. You think I don't know that? Goes without sayin'. Never been a man and his grandson close as we are.

JEFFREY: *(again, sitting next to BOB)* Look, uh, I really didn't fight my way through that Nor'easterner out there to talk about Grandmother and Benjamin.

BOB: Y'all on a first name basis now, too, huh?

JEFFREY: What – ?

BOB: Benjamin. You called that old man Benjamin.

JEFFREY: Grandpop, I've only known him since I was seven years old.

(BOB looks at him a moment.)

BOB: Right ... What am I thinking about? ... And he's done right by you all these years, too ... anybody that got eyes in they head can see that. I'll give old Benright that.

JEFFREY: Wainwright –

BOB: More than I coulda done. 'Course he had a education, not like me.

JEFFREY: He's not exactly what you'd call educated.

BOB: He had some trainin', didn't he? Had to go to undertaker school or somethin'. You got to be licensed to do that kinda work. Built himself that business, didn't he? Everytime somebody kicks the bucket his cash register rings. Dying ain't ever going outa style, you know –

(JEFFREY stands up, moves to the desk.)

JEFFREY: Yeah, and it's not exactly seasonal, either.
BOB: Now what's the matter with you?
JEFFREY: I didn't come here to get you upset.

(He looks to the Bay window.)

BOB: Upset? Who's upset? Look, boy. I'm a man, full grown. And I'm not afraid to give the devil himself his due. In fact, I'm thankful, real thankful. Your Grandmama and her husband, they've done right by you. No sense in gettin' all caught up in a lot of old time mishaps ... No sir, when I look at you I say to myself, I am lookin' at the future, the future ... *(JEFFREY sees the glare of automobile headlights flash across the Bay window)* C'mon – you ain't hardly touched this stuff – *(BOB picks up JEFFREY's drink, stands up, crosses to him; JEFFREY turns to him and, rather reluctantly, takes the glass)* – the future: let's drink to that on this Christmas Eve 'stead o' talkin' about a lotta old stuff ... Yeah, whatever happened to get you where you are today was good. Look at you. Look like a regular All-American black prince or somethin'. *(he toasts)* Hope you live forever and I never die. *(he downs his drink)* Hmm. That feels like another.

(He pours another for himself.)

JEFFREY: Grandpop ... It's your daughter that I've come to talk to you about.
BOB: Your mother ... ?
JEFFREY: You have another daughter that I don't know about?

(BOB sits down in the chair by the fire.)

BOB: Thought you said, you didn't come here to get me upset. You know we don't have much to do with each other.

JEFFREY: I know ... Grandpop, she's in a little trouble.

BOB: Is that supposed to be news? When was she ever not in trouble ... ? *(JEFFREY observes him a moment)* She call you?

JEFFREY: Yeah ... she called ... she's, uh losing her apartment after the new year ... she doesn't have any place to stay ... *(moving to him)* Grandpop, I want you to talk to her.

BOB: Let's not take this Christmas business too far, Jeffrey.

JEFFREY: *(crossing to the fireplace)* I told her about the new house in Virginia –

(BOB laughs bitterly.)

BOB: Humph, you think your mother is gonna go sit up in the country someplace ... with me? You don't know her very well, do you? But then how could you? She give you up when you were not much more than four years old. Party-girl. Couldn't be tied down to no crumb-crusher –

JEFFREY: *(sharply and crossing SC)* I thought we were sticking to the future. *(BOB looks at him)* Grandmother has told me that story just about every time I did something she didn't like ... Presumably, to remind me that failure and shame was truly mother's milk to me ... and therefore total worthlessness would always be just around the corner, waiting for me ... *(he laughs lightly and moves DSL)* and I'd have to work extra hard to find a convenient side street to avoid it ... Sorry, but I think you can see why I'm a little tired of that story.

BOB: Yeah, it's a tired story. Very tired. Makes me tired just to think about it ... but I still don't want to talk to your mother; she'll find a place. She's made out just fine without me all these years and she can keep on doin' it.

JEFFREY: She wants to see you.

BOB: You sure? Or you talked her into wanting to see me?

JEFFREY: Is she supposed to keep on paying for what she did forever? Is that how it's supposed to be? Grandpop, you'd give a stray dog a home, but not your daughter. What kind of sense does that make?

BOB: It don't make no sense at all, Jeffrey ... except it's the way things are ... and me talkin' to your mother won't change that ... it's the way things are.

(JEFFREY glances to the window.)

JEFFREY: I think she's outside.

BOB: What – ?

JEFFREY: I was supposed to meet her here. A car just pulled up. A Benz. I think she's in it ...

BOB: Boy, you expect too much of me.

JEFFREY: I'll go tell her to come in ... okay ... ?

*(There's a silence; BOB steels himself; JEFFREY leaves the
 room.)*

BOB: Jeffrey ... ?

*(He's gone ... BOB slowly stands and stares out into space ...
 Lights fade.)*
(End of Scene.)

Scene Two

(About ten minutes later.)
*(LYDIA TOWNSEND is standing, leaning against the desk.
She's impatiently puffing on a cigarette. She's about
forty-five. Tightly styled wavy hair gives her an almost
Latin look. A broad mouth, turned down at its corners,
reinforces this impression. Determined drinking and
bouts with various drugs have hardened her once
beautiful face into a kind of vacant cruelty. Her clothing
is expensive, yet something about her looks cheap,
ostentatious. A bit too much gold adorns her ears, neck
and wrists.)*
*(Tentatively, she again puffs her cigarette; ashes fall on her
fur coat; anxiously, she knocks them away ...)*

LYDIA: Shit! ... ga'damn ...

*(She looks for an ashtray as JEFFREY enters carrying two
cups of coffee.)*

JEFFREY: Got you some coffee.

(He continues to the desk.)

LYDIA: They got any ashtrays in this joint?
JEFFREY: I'll see if there's one in the kitchen.

*(He puts the coffee on the desk; she notices the fireplace,
starts to it.)*

LYDIA: Never mind ... he comin' down?

JEFFREY: In a minute. *(she crushes out the cigarette underfoot on the fireplace floor)* Why don't you take off your coat?

(He crosses to her, helps her remove her coat.)

LYDIA: What's he doin' up there?
JEFFREY: Getting dressed, I think. He was in his pajamas.

(She crosses to her handbag on the desk.)

LYDIA: *(innocently)* What th' fuck's he gettin' dressed up for? *(JEFFREY looks at her a moment)* What's the matter?
JEFFREY: Nothin' ...

(He starts to the foyer with her coat.)

LYDIA: Wait a minute ...

(She removes a small flask from the coat.)

JEFFREY: I uh, guess he wanted to be presentable. *(he continues to the foyer)* When was the last time you two saw each other?
LYDIA: *(pouring whiskey in her coffee)* Huh?
JEFFREY: I said, when was the last time –
LYDIA: Oh – don't remember. Long time.
JEFFREY: Maybe he just wants to impress you.
LYDIA: Yeah, now I'll tell one. Like hell he does ... *(she caps the whiskey flask)* Here, put that back for me, willya ... ?

(he quickly takes the flask, starts back to the foyer) He live here? This is a church, ain't it?

JEFFREY: A rectory. Grandpop's the Sexton.

LYDIA: What kinda gig is that?

(He re-enters the room watching her closely.)

JEFFREY: He looks after things I guess; fixes them when they break.

LYDIA: Oh, you mean he's the super. Yeah, your Grandfather could always do any fuckin' thing with his hands.

(She sits again, lights another cigarette.)

JEFFREY: Well, I guess that's one way to put it ... He's got a nice little apartment upstairs. Free. I don't think they pay him much. But when you don't have to pay rent I guess you don't need that much.

LYDIA: Hmm. *(she sips the spiked coffee. Again, he watches her a moment)* Why do keep lookin' at me like that?

JEFFREY: Like what?

LYDIA: You now what I'm talkin' about.

JEFFREY: *(he smiles)* I don't know. Maybe I'm looking at you "like that," mother, because, because it's Christmas Eve ... or perhaps its just that I haven't seen you in nine years ... my Junior High School graduation, wasn't it?

LYDIA: *(standing up)* Yeah, right, but please, kid, no trips down memory lane, okay? Dealin' with that old man up there is gonna be fuckin' tough enough.

(She moves to the doorway; he laughs defensively.)

JEFFREY: *(sitting in the chair by the fireplace)* Yeah, sure ... uh, Mother, you uh think maybe you could drop some of the more colorful aspects of your speech when you talk to Grandpop?

LYDIA: You mean, don't curse?

JEFFREY: Yes.

LYDIA: Look, let me tell you somethin': your Grandpop, as you call him, knows me and he knows my ga'damn mouth. And I'm not about to make myself over for nobody, okay? ... *(she goes for her coffee)* Sorry, kid, couldn't do that shit if I tried.

JEFFREY: You know, it would be all right if you called me Jeffrey. It's my name ... and it's a bit more specific than kid. After all, Grandmother says you gave it to me.

LYDIA: I did? Shit.

JEFFREY: So she says.

LYDIA: Guess I did ... Oh yeah, now I remember. Named you after that movie star: Jeff Chandler. You ever heard of him?

JEFFREY: No. 'Fraid not.

LYDIA: Think th' muthafucka died kinda young. Sad. But he was real good though ... I named you Jeff. Your Grandmother stretched it to Jeffrey ... Shit, seems like a hundred fuckin' years ago ...

(She moves to the window.)

JEFFREY: No. Just about twenty-three – then uh, maybe you'd like it better if you called me Jeff.

LYDIA: Would you like it better?

(He hesitates.)

JEFFREY: No, not particularly.

LYDIA: Hmm. Thought not ... *(she puffs her cigarette)* So ... you got a woman?

JEFFREY: *(he grins)* No, not particularly.

LYDIA: You like girls, don't you?

JEFFREY: I'm not gay if that's what you mean.

LYDIA: Good. Your Grandmother, she's from the old school, she'd have a fuckin' shit-fit about somethin' like that.

JEFFREY: Yeah. Guess she would ... And what about you? Would you have uh ... a fit?

LYDIA: Me? It's none o' my business. But for a young dude that looks like you, it'd be a terrible ga'damn waste.

JEFFREY: Well ... thanks for the compliment, mother ... uh that was a compliment, wasn't it?

LYDIA: No, I just calls 'em like I sees 'em, that's all ... Look, I think you better call me Lydia.

(She moves to the desk, gets another cigarette, then moves again to the doorway.)

JEFFREY: Sure ... Well ... at least we've got that straight. I'm Jeffrey and you're Lydia – and at the moment I am seeing a number of young ladies, but there's no one in particular.

LYDIA: *(distractedly)* Sure, sure, just playin' the field a little, huh? Shit, nothin' wrong with that at your age.

JEFFREY: *(he laughs, stands up)* Exactly ... well ... I guess that adequately covers the last nine years.

(She looks at him, sits down again, sips the coffee.)

LYDIA: You know, sometimes you sound like a ga'damn rich white boy. What you studyin'?

JEFFREY: *(he laughs)* And now you sound like Grandpop. Of course he likes the way I talk, pretends he doesn't, but he has a lot of fun with it. What about you? I mean, it doesn't bother you, does it?

LYDIA: Kid – Jeffrey, it doesn't make a damn bit of difference what I like as far as you're concerned. Never has. And that's probably all for the best if you know what I mean.

JEFFREY: Yeah ... Well, in answer to your question, my BA was in Philosophy. I graduated last May. I'm now concentrating on Poetry and Dramatic Literature.

LYDIA: All that gonna do you any fuckin' good?

JEFFREY: I hope it already has done me some good, philosophically speaking.

LYDIA: How you gonna make a livin'?

JEFFREY: Teach, probably.

LYDIA: No too much cash in that, is it?

JEFFREY: Enough, I hope.

(She gets up again, moves to doorway, then to the window.)

LYDIA: Hmm. Well, long as you doin' what you want to do ... Shit, wish he'd come on down here! Plato's gon' freeze his ass off out in that car. Betcha he's sittin' there without the ga'damn motor runnin' – man can't stand to waste a ounce o' gas.

JEFFREY: Plato? His name's Plato?

LYDIA: Yeah. So what?

JEFFREY: I just said my BA was in Philosophy ...

LYDIA: Yeah?

(He hesitates.)

JEFFREY: Never mind. Well, I'd better go ask Plato in to join our little Christmas Eve symposium.

LYDIA: No, leave his dumb ass out there – *(JEFFREY sits again in the armchair)* Listen, is your Grandfather dressin' for a ga'damn ball or what? *(BOB enters; JEFFREY sees him)* What th' fuck's he doing up there – ?

JEFFREY: Grandpop.

LYDIA: *(turning to BOB)* Well ... speak o' th' devil ...

BOB: Lydia. *(he looks at her a moment)* I see your mouth's still draggin' the gutter.

(She glances at JEFFREY.)

LYDIA: Yeah ... well ... I'm, I'm outa cash, Pop ... I finally hit bottom in good old New York, New York. I need to get my ass outa –

BOB: It's been ten years. Can't you even say hello before you start beggin'.

(She looks at BOB, then moves to the desk.)

LYDIA: Still tellin' me what to say and when to say it. *(to JEFFREY)* Toldya this shit wouldn't work.

BOB: A simple hello. That too much for you?

(She sighs, looks for a place to dump her cigarette.)

LYDIA: Kid – uh, Jeffrey, you said you was gon' get me a astray?

JEFFREY: Yeah, sure.

(JEFFREY and BOB exchange glances. JEFFREY exits; LYDIA sits down.)

BOB: Lydia, I said –

LYDIA: Hello ... How's that?

BOB: Lydia, I mean to be civil. I sat upstairs thinking about how to greet you, and I made up my mind to be civil.

LYDIA: Well, ain't that fuckin' grand.

BOB: But not if you gon' give free reign to your mouth like that. If you gonna do that you might as well take your behind on outa here right now – !

LYDIA: Okay ... I can't promise nothin' but I'll try ... How you been, Pop?

BOB: That's better ... I been okay. You?

LYDIA: Not too good. *(she laughs lightly)* That's why th' fuc – that's why I'm here – you see, I'm tryin'.

BOB: Your health all right?

LYDIA: Yeah, Pop. My health's fine.

BOB: You look like you stop takin' that stuff.

LYDIA: Seven years ago.

BOB: *(sitting down in the armchair)* Good. God knows, you'd be dead by now if you was still –

LYDIA: Tell me about it ... still drink my liquor though.

(She sips her coffee.)

BOB: Have you spoken to your mother lately?

LYDIA: No. Have you?

BOB: You should do your mother the courtesy of stayin' in touch. That's the least you could do ... she did raise your son for you.

LYDIA: Yeah, she did do that, didn't she? ... She don't wanna hear from me.

BOB: How you know that? You just said, you don't keep in touch.

LYDIA: *(a short bitter laugh)* You don't wanna hear from me, Pop. Why th' hell would she?

(JEFFREY enters with an ashtray and his coat crossing to LYDIA.)

JEFFREY: Here you go ... Lydia.

LYDIA: Thanks –

BOB: Where you goin'?

JEFFREY: I'm gonna take a little walk –

BOB: A walk! Now, boy – ?

JEFFREY: *(putting on his coat)* I'm gonna sit outside in the car with mother's ... uh, escort. Seems he doesn't know that the heater only works when the car's running.

BOB: Just what are you talking about? *(to LYDIA)* What's he talkin' about? Somebody waitin' for you out there?

LYDIA: That's what the young man said.

BOB: Another one o' your Number Runner friends?

(JEFFREY starts to the foyer.)

LYDIA: Numbers? No more real cash in that, Pop. Lotto just about sent that shit to a early grave.

JEFFREY: Yell for help if you need a referee.

(He exits.)

BOB: Jeffrey ... ? *(he's gone)* Is that supposed to be funny?

LYDIA: If it is, you damn sure ain't laughin'.

(He looks at her a moment, sits down.)

BOB: Well, Girlie, what can I do for you?

LYDIA: He's a kinda pretty thing, ain't he? ... Never knew he'd grow up like that. Mama did a good job believe it or not.

BOB: Yeah. No thanks to you.

LYDIA: Oh, I see we gon' pickup right where we left off, after ten ga'damn years –

BOB: Just statin' a fact, that's all.

LYDIA: That's right. Run my ass down –

BOB: Give that boy up when he was four years old –

LYDIA: *(a tiresome litany)* Yeah, y' got that right. I'm guilty, the worse ga'damn mother that's ever lived in this tired ass world –

BOB: Lydia –

LYDIA: And, a fucked up daughter, too. Worse scuzzy ass bitch that ever –

BOB: LYDIA! ... This is a church, Girlie.

LYDIA: Just thought I'd get all that out the way, and save you the trouble ...

(A short awkward silence.)

BOB: Well, anyway, it's good to know there's still somethin' decent enough in you that don't allow you to look in that boy's face and not feel somethin' ...

LYDIA: I may be ignorant, but I ain't blind.

BOB: You've changed some. Looks like it might be for the better.

LYDIA: I been through a lotta shit, Pop –

BOB: Lydia –

LYDIA: Yeah, I know. It's a church. *(she drinks again quickly, then stands up)* Pop, look, I uh, I need –

BOB: You know, I never did understand you.

LYDIA: That makes two of us. I never did understand me neither –

BOB: Pretty girl, beautiful! Better lookin' than all the girls you came up with. Had some brains, too –

LYDIA: Beauty is as beauty does. Isn't that what you usta say? Look, Pop –

BOB: But I guess if you can see something in that boy, maybe –

LYDIA: Pop! I gotta get outa New York. Coolie's trial is comin' up, and I –

BOB: Coolie? Who's Coolie? That man outside?

(She thinks a moment.)

LYDIA: Who's Coolie? Wish I could say that ... *(to herself)* All of a sudden, it really don't matter who th' fuck he is, not any more ... *(to him)* Pop, I need about six months to get myself together. Maybe I could get a little job down there –

BOB: Who is Coolie?

LYDIA: *(carefully)* Coolie Jenkins.

BOB: Where've I heard that name before ... ?

LYDIA: Pop –

BOB: Wait a minute, you mean the fool that runs half the drugs in Harlem? You mixed up with him? Well, Girlie, you have come up in the world. Thought they just put his behind in jail and threw the key away.

LYDIA: We was together.

(He looks at her and shakes his head.)

BOB: Together. Somehow I know that don't mean married.

LYDIA: No. It don't ... we hooked up 'bout eight years ago ... He helped me ... helped me break my habit ... Pop, there's people that's gonna fight over his business; they gonna fight and die over it. And I don't wanna get messed up in that shit.

BOB: I thought you told Jeffrey you were supposed to be losin' your apartment.

LYDIA: He's had enough bad news about me. I didn't want to give him no more.

(She goes to the window; he pauses.)

BOB: Well, ain't this somethin'. So you stopped being a dope fiend and got into the business end, huh?

LYDIA: I don't know nothin' about Coolie's business! He never told me nothin'. I'll swear that shit on a stack o' Bibles.

BOB: The fruits of his business is hangin' all round your neck, Lydia.

LYDIA: I wasn't in it! He didn't want me in it! ... *(again, to herself)* It was crazy, Pop: outa all the men I been with, I think he's the first one really cared somethin' about me ... humph, for all the fuckin' good it did. *(she moves to her father)* No, all I know about his business is what I read in the papers, and that's the ga'damn truth ...

BOB: Good. If that's so, you ain't got nothin' to worry 'bout.

LYDIA: What? You think these money-hungry niggers'll believe that. Pop, they'll get me involved in this shitin'-ass war they 'bout to start sure as I'm standin' here.

BOB: You think these people you 'fraid of don't know how to get to Virginia?

LYDIA: They'll leave me alone, if I can get outa New York. You see, that means I can't be runnin' to Coolie tellin' him everythin' they doin'. I can't be on nobody's side. I'll be out of it, free and clear.

(He considers this a moment.)

BOB: And this man outside in the car, who's he?

LYDIA: Oh that's just Plato, Coolie's dumb ass brother. If Coolie does the time, and believe me, he will, Plato will be the first one in the ga'damn morgue ... *(he stands up)* Well. That's the whole sad-ass story.

(She sits again in one of the folding chairs.)

BOB: Yeah, and you got your only son sittin' out there with a known criminal, a man you say other criminals are huntin'.

(He starts to the doorway.)

LYDIA: Pop, please, the kid'll be all right. Nobody's gonna make a move until they're sure Coolie's out the way.

BOB: *(getting his coat)* How can you be so sure about that, Lydia?

LYDIA: Shit, you think I'da let him go out there if it was dang –

BOB: Girlie, I don't know what you might do!

(He grabs his muffler.)

LYDIA: *(angrily)* Right! Go get him! The dumb bitch sent his young-ass out there to be iced – !

(The off stage foyer door is heard opening.)

BOB: Jeffrey ... ?

(JEFFREY appears in the doorway removing and hanging up his coat.)

JEFFREY: Brrr! Cold out there ... Going someplace, Grandpop?

BOB: Huh? Uh, no, I was, I was uh just comin' out to see how you was doin'.

(He removes his coat, hangs it up.)

JEFFREY: Oh. Well I was about to freeze my ga'noolies off sitting in that car with m'man Plato. *(enters the room, retrieves his sherry glass from the desk)* You were right, the brother doesn't intend to waste an ounce of gas. And he's a little too big to be forcibly convinced to the contrary.

BOB: You see anybody else out there?

JEFFREY: *(crossing to the small table by the fire)* No, not a soul. But Plato and I did have a short but very interesting talk ... He says, "the cold is only a state of mind."

(He pours himself a sherry.)

BOB: He must be a fool.

JEFFREY: Maybe. Maybe not. Think about it: A man named Plato, sits in a car on Lenox Avenue on Christmas Eve in the twilight of the twentieth century and says: "the cold is only a state of mind." Is he discussing the transcendent powers of the mind, practicing, extending even, the twenty-five hundred year old insights of a Greek philosopher who just happens to be his namesake? *(to BOB)* Is this merely millenial coincidence? – *(to LYDIA)* of course Plato the Younger never heard of his venerated Athenian forebear; his mama picked the name out of a book – *(moving to the window)* Or is the great, singular hum of universal consciousness revealing itself, the unknown yet knowable truth, the changing yet unchangeable truth, the truth beyond all pairs of opposites? – *(he raises the glass to the window, toasting Plato)* "There are more things in heaven and earth than are dreamt of in your philosophy, Horatio" – *(to LYDIA and BOB)* Or is Plato the younger just a mis-named brother rappin' to pass the time? Is he, as Grandpop says quite plaintively, "a fool" trying to convince a cullud college boy that he's not as dumb as everybody thinks he is ... ? Maybe ... *(almost mystically)* Yet, folks, as far as I could see, he was not cold. *(they look at him dumbfounded)* Well, anyway, what round is this? Any decision yet? *(he sips his sherry; they are *unable to reply; JEFFREY goes to refill his glass)* No? You need more time. Okay, I'll take this upstairs and wait for the outcome ... Oh, if I may be allowed to add my two cents: Grandpop, I can't see you spending the rest of your days alone in some little house in Virginia, and mother – you'll excuse me, Lydia, if, for the moment at least, I call you mother. After Plato, I've a sudden need to cling to biological realities, philosophic ones are so very slippery – Mother, maybe, just maybe, it's about time you uh ... sat up in the country for awhile.

(He exits upstairs; they pause a moment.)

LYDIA: *(moving to the doorway)* Is he all right? Where the hell he learn to talk like that?

BOB: Not from you that's for sure. Now you see what you been missin'. You see what you had there, what you brought into this world ... ? *(she doesn't respond)* You ain't even interested. All you can think about is yourself.

LYDIA: *(pained)* I toldya before, I might be ignorant, but I ain't blind.

BOB: Yeah, and I heard you. Only now it's a little late in the day ... and you've missed your chance with that boy.

(She thinks a moment.)

LYDIA: Maybe not ... Pop, he wants us to –

BOB: It don't matter what he wants. It's too late! ... It's like I always told you, you lay down with dogs and you're gonna get up smellin' like one ... Girlie, I can't help you. You made your bed now I'm afraid you gonna have to lie in it.

LYDIA: Well, damn if you ain't still full o' all those old time coloured folks sayin's. "Girl you ain't got the sense you was born with." "Beauty is only skin deep." "If you keep it up, you're gonna find yourself gettin' up off the floor." Shit, you oughta write 'em down, so they won't be lost to history.

BOB: Believe me, I wish I could help, but I just can't –

(She moves away to the desk.)

LYDIA: Right! I heard you the first time. No help.

BOB: You forty-five years old and you been runnin' these streets like somethin' wild, since you was sixteen ... Girlie, I don't know how either of us can do much about that now.

LYDIA: Look, I don't think you understand. These sonsabitches mean business. It's more cash at stake here than you ever thought about ... Pop. Have I bothered you? Have I asked you for anything in ten muthafuckin' years? No. I have stayed to myself, kept all my shit to myself. I know how you and mama feel about me and I been ga'damn scarce. But this ain't no stage joke. Pop, they gonna hurt people.

BOB: I can't protect you no more. I'm too old. You not a child no more. You got to reap what you –

LYDIA: Please! ... Don't give me no more of them ga'damn sayings. You can go through life quotin' shit, thinking it'll make everything okay if you want, but right now that don't do me no ga'damn good! *(She sits down, tries to compose herself, lights another cigarette)* Well ... looks like I turned out just like you always said I would. You started tellin' me I wasn't goin' to be nothin' from time you and mama broke up.

BOB: Lydia, it don't make much sense now to go back to all that old time –

LYDIA: Well that's what you said, wasn't it? And that's when you started sayin' it! I remember it like it was yesterday ... Always wondered why I had to be punished because she left.

BOB: That had nothin' to do with it. You started actin' like a crazy person. I tried to tell you what path you was travellin' –

LYDIA: Right! You had one o' them shitin'-ass sayin's to fit every occasion ... then you put me out.

BOB: That's a lie. I sent you to your mother. A man can't raise a girl-child without a woman's –

LYDIA: You knew she never had no time for me, not even when we was all together. Then, after, she was too fuckin' busy lookin' for a new husband.

BOB: That's not true. Your mother loved you. Always did.

LYDIA: No, Pop, you always wanted her to! ... why did you send me to her?

BOB: She's your mother. A young girl oughta be with her mother. I had them two jobs, super in the day, the automat at night. I couldn't keep track o' you. 'Specially the way you started actin'. What was I supposed to do? I sent you to her and she did the best she could. But, Girlie, you were unmanageable – it suits you to forget that part. Never mind how you was runnin' after every narrow behind Jack-in-the-box walkin'. Sixteen years old and behavin' like anybody's full grown huzzy. Yeah, it suits you to forget that ... What could she do with you? What could anybody do?

LYDIA: *(standing up)* Well I'll be ga'damn, you still

takin' up for her. She's on her third husband, and you still takin' up for her.

BOB: I ain't takin' up for nobody. I'm just tryin' to tell the truth!

LYDIA: Oh, so now you after the truth. Well, don't stop there. *(moving to him)* Go all th' fuckin' way! Get into that truth about how you always cared more about her than you did me –

BOB: I didn't, Lydia, I didn't –

LYDIA: About how you was always runnin' after her, seein' where she was goin', who she was with, 'cause you was afraid you was gonna lose her to some nigger with more cash ... Tell it! Run it on down! Don't clean the shit up. Let it all hang out! ... Tell th' truth 'bout how you thought if you sent me to her it'd keep her from gettin' another ga'damn man!

BOB: Lydia, please –

LYDIA: My mother was a high-class 1940s Sugar Hill party-girl, and Imma low-class 1960s Lenox Avenue party-girl. Like mother, like daughter. Now that's the muthafuckin' truth!

(A short silence.)

BOB: Lydia, people ain't perfect, but just look what she's done for your son.

LYDIA: Guilt! The bitch did it outa fuckin' guilt!

BOB: *(standing, crossing to her)* Lydia, please, stop this, stop hatin' your mama; it can't do you no good, Girlie ... and it's hurt you enough already. Who did what to who, and when, and where and why they did it, can't help either of us too much right now ... can it?

(She thinks a moment.)

LYDIA: *(quietly)* No, Pop ... you're right ... it damn sure can't ...

BOB: And she did put a lot into that boy upstairs, for whatever the reason. Got to give her that. Spent oo-gobs o' money on his education from the time he was in grade school. You got to give her that, Girlie.

LYDIA: I wouldn't be too sure about where the cash came from if I was you, Pop ... Where'd the kid put my coat?

BOB: In the hall – *(she starts to the foyer)* What you talkin' about?

(She stops.)

LYDIA: Just wouldn't be to sure about it, that's all ... I gotta go.

(She goes for her coat.)

BOB: Lydia ... Lydia what you gonna do now?

LYDIA: Take my chances. *(referring to her coat and jewelry and moving to her handbag on the desk)* I'll pawn some of this shit. Get me enough for a bus ticket to somewhere and a few nights in a cheap hotel. Don't know what the hell I'm gonna do after that. But I'll think of somethin' ...

BOB: Don't you want to say goodbye to your son?

(She looks at him a moment.)

LYDIA: Yeah. I think I do.

(BOB goes to the doorway as LYDIA sits again on one of the folding chairs.)

BOB: Jeffrey ... Jeffrey ... C'mon down your mother is leavin'. *(he turns to her)* Lydia, I want you to know if there was any way that I could –

LYDIA: Pop! ... don't explain nothin'. You said no. Let that be it, okay ... ?

(BOB looks at her, nods yes; JEFFREY enters; he looks at BOB who turns away. He looks to LYDIA.)

JEFFREY: You're leaving? ... Then I guess it's all settled ... ? Grandpop? ... You're taking her with you when you go down, right?

(BOB hesitates.)

BOB: I told you before, boy, I didn't think I could do that.

JEFFREY: Well, why not? She's drug free. She drinks a little but then so do you. The two of you could have a ball. What's the problem ... ? *(BOB doesn't reply)* Okay. So where are we now? Back in 1962?

LYDIA: Kid –

BOB: Jeffrey, I know, come hell or high-water, she's your mother and, believe me, I'm proud that you takin' up for her like this –

JEFFREY: That's got nothin' to do with it. I hardly know her. You and Grandmother made sure of that. The fact that she's your daughter is more to the point. I'm asking you to treat her like she's your daughter, not some stranger off the street!

BOB: Jeffrey –

LYDIA: Let me talk to him, Pop ... by myself.

BOB: Lydia, what good – ?

LYDIA: I ain't gon' teach him how to snort coke; I just want to talk to him. Look, you been wantin' us together all these years, right? So now you can give us a few ga'damn minutes.

(BOB looks at her and JEFFREY a moment.)

BOB: I'll go make us some more coffee.

(He exits.)

LYDIA: Kid-uh, Jeffrey, I uh, didn't tell you the real reason I havta get outa town ... Didn't want to give you no more bad news about me if you know what I mean – see I know your Grandmother been workin' over time in the bad-news-about-Lydia department all these years. To her, I'm the worse bitch that ever took breath.

JEFFREY: So why do you have to leave the city? What is it – ?

LYDIA: Let me finish ... Well, mostly she was right. I know she only told her side of it, but mostly she was right.

JEFFREY: For once, I'd like to hear your side of it.

LYDIA: I don't want to get into it. But I'm in much worse trouble than I told you, and your Grandfather don't want nothin' to do with it ... And he's right, too; he's too old to get himself mixed up in this mess.

JEFFREY: Maybe I can help. You ever thought of that?

LYDIA: No-no. I definitely ain't gettin' you involved in this shit. You got to leave it alone, Jeffrey ... *(JEFFREY looks at her, then sits again in the armchair)* Tell me, why you so ga'damn worried about me? Like you said, you don't hardly know me. And I told you before, that's the way it oughta be.

JEFFREY: I'm worried about how my Grandfather is treating his daughter.

LYDIA: *(she smiles)* Look, you can tell him that shit, but don't hand it to me, okay? I wasn't born yesterday. *(she stands up, moves to him)* I see the way you look at me ... that big-ass brain just workin', lookin' for somethin', somethin' that's missin', like it gon' find out one little thing that's gonna make everything all right ... well, forget it, baby, that ain't gon' happen no how, no way. All you got to understand is that your Grandfather is for you, give his life for you – your Grandmother, too ... and I fucked up with them before you was even thought about.

JEFFREY: I still want to hear your side of it. I think I'm entitled to that.

LYDIA: Jeffrey, baby, believe me, that wouldn't change a thing.

(He looks at her a moment.)

JEFFREY: I think ... I like "baby" even better than I like Jeffrey.

(She forces back a tearful smile.)

LYDIA: *(crossing to the desk again)* Aw, c'mon, now, Jeffrey, don't put me through some ga'damn sentimental shit now ... I gotta walk outa here in a minute and I'm never gon' see your face again.

JEFFREY: Why can't you see me again? Because Grandpop wouldn't want it and Grandmother wouldn't? I'm an adult. They can't tell me who –

LYDIA: I wouldn't want it ... wouldn't do either of us a damn bit of good. Like your Grandfather said, it's much too late in the day. *(she pauses, moves SC)* Well. I wanted to say thanks. See, you did help me. You got me to see my father, somethin' I wanted to do for years. I kinda missed that old man a little. Didn't know it till I saw him. I remember how much I usta look up to him – oh, yeah I usta think he was the most important thing since electric lights ... I liked remembering that time. It was a good time ... Thankya, Jeffrey ... Well. Guess Plato's a ga'damn block o' ice by now.

(She starts to the foyer.)

JEFFREY: Mother. *(she stops)* You loved, Grandpop, didn't you ... ?

LYDIA: *(she hesitates)* Still do in my own crazy-ass kinda way ... *(she looks at him a moment)* Jeffrey, I gotta go.

JEFFREY: Would you give me a lift to the train station on 125th?

LYDIA: Sure, but I thought you was gonna stay over – look, you not blaming your Grandfather for nothin', are you –

JEFFREY: No. I just want to get back up to school tonight. I've got a paper that's overdue. Shoulda handed it in before the Christmas break.

(She looks at him a moment.)

LYDIA: It won't do you no good to blame him for nothin' ... I'll be outside ... *(she starts into the foyer)* Better go get this dumb muthafucka to turn that heater on.

(She exits.)
(The foyer door is heard shutting ... JEFFREY thinks a moment; BOB enters with the coffee.)

BOB: She gone ... ?
JEFFREY: "There have been losses, but there also have been gains. The people have suffered, but the people have endured. Martin Luther King, Jr., is right in a sense that transcends grammar and statistics when he quotes the ungrammatical truth of an old preacher: 'Lord, we ain't what we oughta be; we ain't what we wanna be; we ain't what we gonna be; but thank God, we ain't what we was'."
BOB: *(putting the coffee tray on the desk)* Boy, what are you –
JEFFREY: It's from your book, Grandpop. *Before The Mayflower,* the end of chapter 13, appropriately titled: "We Cannot Escape History." I memorized it years ago. It seemed important somehow ... I never suspected it would one day help me understand my mother.

(A silence.)

BOB: I guess you never gonna forgive me for this, huh?
JEFFREY: Forgive? I'm not in a position to forgive anybody. I've just been taking all of my ... young life. But I guess that's what you do when you're young, huh? Take a lot. And hope you can find a way to live up to all that's been

given ... look, I'm going back up to school. I've got some work to do. Lydia – *(he looks to the door where she's just exited)* No. Mother is waiting ... *(again to BOB)* They're gonna drop me off at the train station.

(He stands up.)

BOB: So you takin' her side, aren't you?
JEFFREY: Grandpop, please. There are no sides.
BOB: Did she tell you the reason why she gotta get outa the city?
JEFFREY: What are you getting upset about? She's just dropping me at the station –
BOB: Did she tell you? No! Damn right she didn't – looka here, got me cursing now, too –
JEFFREY: I don't care what she's done.
BOB: What do you mean, you don't care? You'd care if you knew.
JEFFREY: Well is she a murderer? Did she kill somebody?

(He moves away SL to window.)

BOB: Yeah! ... in a manner of speaking. Jeffrey, boy, your mother was livin' with the biggest drug man in Harlem. She swears she ain't got nothin' to do with his business, well maybe she don't. But she's takin' his money. Money he got from the young, black, walkin' dead that he sells that poison to. Yes! That's murder, ain't it? She let herself get tied up with that kinda man.
JEFFREY: A woman needs a man and a man needs a woman. Isn't that what you always used to say?

BOB: No woman needs that kinda man.

JEFFREY: *(trying not to explode)* Well just who did you expect her to get, the second vice-president of Ebony magazine? It doesn't take a genius to see that my mother has spent most of her life surviving on the streets! ... and, though no one thinks I'm old enough to hear the goddamn story, I somehow deeply suspect that you and Grandmother have something to do with that!

(A silence.)

BOB: Yeah, you're right. We definitely had something to do with it.

(He sits down.)

JEFFREY: And one more thing: All the private schools and college tuition, before I was able to get any full scholarships, she paid for it ...

BOB: She said somethin' about – No, Jeffrey, she's just making that up to –

JEFFREY: Benjamin told me that ... right after I graduated. He said he wasn't supposed to – Grandmother didn't want any sudden alliance between me and her eternally worthless daughter – but he thought I had a right to know at least one good thing about my mother ...

BOB: You coulda let me know that. I wouldna let it get back to your Grandmama.

JEFFREY: I couldn't actually be sure of that, could I? You both seemed so totally agreed on the need to keep your Grandson and his mother apart ... Anyway, that street money, that walkin' dead money, as you call it, paid to educate this young black man of great expectations: all his wonderful academic assets have been produced by the four horsemen of every black ghetto's apocalypse: heroine, cocaine, crack, and, most of all, despair ... Grandpop, I ... I just don't know how I'm going to deal with that. I don't know ... But then that's not my mother's problem; the way I look at it, under the circumstances, she just did the best she could ... *(he pauses a moment)* they're waiting. You have a good Christmas. I'll give you a call tomorrow.

(He starts to the doorway.)

BOB: Maybe we all did the best we could ... *(JEFFREY stops and slowly turns as BOB continues)* Jeffrey, long as I been here in this world, I still don't understand it, I don't know why things go so hard with us. It seems like everything walkin' on two legs that puts on they pants the same way was born to suffer. You try and you try, and you try some more. And you can try hard as you damn well please, but things still won't work out, not with people they won't ... Got to get me a plant or a dog, or somethin'.

JEFFREY: But if we don't keep on trying with each other, then what's the point? Why are we all here? Wh-What does it all mean? You want a dog or plant. *(he kneels to his grandfather)* But you're a man ... with a daughter and a grandson. You're human ... and doesn't that mean trying with each other ... suffering, and still trying? *(he sighs deeply, stands up)* Well, anyway, Merry Christmas, Grandpop. I will give you a call. Promise.

(He crosses to the foyer, gets his coat.)

BOB: Jeffrey.
JEFFREY: Yeah ...
BOB: *(standing up)* Tell your mother I said to come in here for a minute please.

(JEFFREY starts to him.)

JEFFREY: Grandpop – ?
BOB: Go on, boy. Do like I said.

(JEFFREY grins broadly and sharply pumps his fist into the air as if at a sporting event.)

JEFFREY: Yes!

(He rushes out ... BOB stands for a moment thinking ...)

BOB:
"Lord, we ain't what we oughta be;
We ain't what we wanna be;
We ain't what we gonna be,
But thank God, we ain't what we was."

(Lights fade as "The Christmas Song" swells ...)

THE END

PROPERTIES:

Cassette Player & Tape, Telephone, Book, Bible, Ashtray, Cigarettes, Lighter, Decanter of Sherry, 2 Sherry glasses, A small whiskey flask, Desk and matching chair, An easy chair, 2 Metal folding chairs, Small table, Tree-styled coatrack, Styrofoam coffee cups, Small upholstery pillow, Small serving tray, Church record books, Bookcase, Cabinet

COSTUMES:

A man's pajamas

Terry-cloth Bathrobe

2 Men's Winter weight outer coats

Woman's Fur Coat

A man's pair of bedroom slippers

Costume Jewelry:
    Gaudy earrings, heavy necklace, bracelet, etc.

2 Men's mufflers

1 Pair of men's shoes

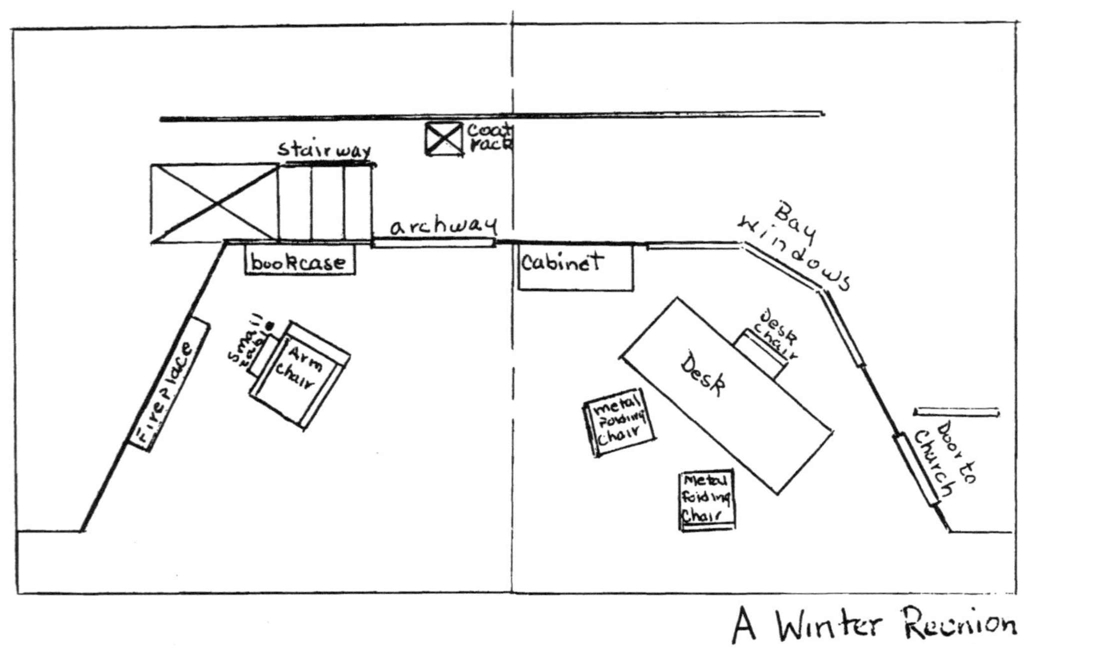

A Winter Reunion
by
Henry Miller
Designed by:
Aiene D. Washington

Off Off Broadway Festival Plays

**The best plays entered in the annual
Off Off Broadway Short Play Festival**

4TH SERIES
An Empty Space   Nothing Immediate   Open Admission

5TH SERIES
Batbrains   Me Too, Then!   ""Hello, Ma!"

6TH SERIES
A Bench at the Edge   Seduction Duet

7TH SERIES
MD 20/20   Passing Fancy

8TH SERIES
Dreamboats   A Change from Routine   Auto-Erotic
Misadventure

9TH SERIES
Now Departing   Something to Eat   The Enchanted Mesa
The Dicks   Piece for an Audition

10TH SERIES
Delta Triangle   Dispatches from Hell   Molly and James
Senior Prom   12:21 p.m.

11TH SERIES
Daddy's Home   Ghost Stories   Recensio   The Ties That Bind

(CONTINUED)

12TH SERIES

The Brannock Device   The Prettiest Girl in Lafayette County
Slivovitz   Two and Twenty

13TH SERIES

Beached   A Grave Encounter   No Problem   Reservations for
Two   Strawberry Preserves   What's a Girl to Do

14TH SERIES

A Blind Date with Mary   Bums   Civilization and Its
Malcontents   Do Over   Tradition 1A

15TH SERIES

The Adventures of Captain Neato-Man   A Chance Meeting
Chateau Rene   Does This Woman Have a Name?   For Anne
The Heartbreak Tour   The Pledge

16TH SERIES

As Angeles Watch   Autumn Leaves   Goods   King of the
Pekinese Yellowtail   Uranium   Way Deep   The Whole Truth
The Winning Number

17TH SERIES

Correct Address   Cowboys, Indians and Waitresses
Homebound   The Road to Nineveh   Your Life Is a Feature
Film

18TH SERIES

How Many to Tango?   Just Thinking   Last Exit Before Toll
Pasquini the Magnificent   Peace in Our Time   The Power and
the Glory   Something Rotten in Denmark   Visiting Oliver

19TH SERIES

Awkward Silence   Cherry Blend with Vanilla   Family Names
Highwire   Nothing in Common   Pizza: A Love Story   The
Spelling Bee

www.ingramcontent.com/pod-product-compliance
Lightning Source LLC
Chambersburg PA
CBHW070322120726
47909CB00008B/2555